SILVER MOON

GREAT NOVELS
OF
EROTIC DOMINATION
AND SUBMISSION

NEW TITLES EVERY MONTH

www.smbooks.co.uk

TO FIND OUT MORE ABOUT OUR READERS' CLUB
WRITE TO;

SILVER MOON READER SERVICES;
Suite 7,
Mayden House,
Long Bennington Business Park,
Newark NG23 5DJ
Tel; 01400283488

YOU WILL RECEIVE A FREE MAGAZINE OF EXTRACTS
FROM OUR EXTENSIVE RANGE OF EROTIC FICTION
ABSOLUTELY FREE. YOU WILL ALSO HAVE THE CHANCE
TO PURCHASE BOOKS WHICH ARE EXCLUSIVE TO OUR
READERS' CLUB

***

NEW AUTHORS ARE WELCOME

Please send submissions to;
The Editor; Silver Moon books
Suite 7Long Bennington Business Park
Newark NG23 5DJ

All characters and events depicted are entirely fictitious; any resemblance to anyone living or dead is entirely coincidental

Mistress Blackheart

by

Francine Whittaker

With thanks to Martin for the encouragement,
and to everyone else who helped

PROLOGUE

Chantel looked down her nose at the naked, quivering wretch kneeling at her feet. Slowly, she swept the back of one white-gloved hand beneath his chin before continuing the movement up the side of his face. Then, adjusting her stance to allow the split in her floor length, white ball gown to fall open, she displayed her smooth, naked leg provocatively, knowing the poor man was slowly being driven mad with desire.

Meanwhile, standing at the back of the small group of semi-clothed women, Ali looked on in awe. After all this time, she still found it incredible that Chantel's authority, not to mention her sexuality, pervaded the very atmosphere of the chateau. The woman was magnificent! With her blonde hair and the elbow-length gloves that were her trademark, she possessed the power to make men and women alike worship her.

The erotic tension in the high-ceilinged room was almost tangible and Ali swallowed hard, fighting to keep the powerful charges that ricocheted through her body in check. Such was her own arousal that she slipped one hand down to rub her clitoris through the gossamer thin panties that barely covered her mound while extracting her breast from the half cup of her black Basque with the other hand. Now, rubbing her clit and tweaking her engorged nipple, she watched as the scene unfolded.

Chantel raised her foot and with the toe of her white, spiked shoe, lifted the man's chin. His hands were bound behind his back and his eyes lowered to the floor. In this place he was nothing but a slave, as docile as a lamb and not the overbearing, fat cat company director who'd checked into the chateau less than a month ago.

When she spoke, Chantel's accent was as thick as the lust in her flat belly.

"Ok, Ladies," she said kicking the powerless man backward so that he fell awkwardly with his legs splayed beneath him, "he's all yours."

The half dozen or so women assembled needed no further encouragement as they surged forward. Some carried canes or whips, while others had nothing but their bare hands with which to exact their particular brand of punishment. They corrected his position, leaning him forward over a tapestry covered footstool.

Within moments his well-rounded backside bore angry, red stripes that had him snivelling, even as he begged for the onslaught to continue. As his penis metamorphosed from a useless, shrivelled appendage to a thick rod of iron, his tormentors released his hands and made him crawl on all fours. While one girl followed behind, every once in a while tapping his balls with the tip of her cane, Ali sat astride him, urging him ever forward with a curious blend of threats and promises.

Watching the proceedings from the sidelines, Chantel raised her hand and, catching Ali's attention at last and beckoned her over.

Grinning like a kid who'd just won a prize at the fair, Ali wiped the back of her hand over her sweaty forehead as she dismounted. Swaying her hips as she invariably did when wearing high heels, Ali approached the 'White Goddess' as Chantel was known to her clients, slaves and even her associates, with due respect.

To Ali's surprise, Chantel drew her close and for a moment the two women were locked in a tight embrace. While they'd often shared and figuratively mopped the floor with slaves, and slept together often, this was the first occasion on which Chantel had shown any tenderness towards her.

The display lasted no more than minutes before Chantel recovered her poise and released her protégé. Leading Ali to a couch, she waited until they were both seated before voicing her thoughts.

"Are you sure you want to do this, Ali? You know you don't have to leave. There will always be a place for you here at the chateau..." she lifted Ali's open hand and held it flat against her own chest, "and here in my heart."

"I know," Ali's confident tone momentarily wavered, "and I thank you for it. I've had some of the best times of my life here with you and love you dearly, but now it's time to move on and put some of what you've taught me into practice. It's time to start up my own 'house of correction'. "

"But why go back to England to do that? What's so important there that you have to leave all this?" Chantel swept her hand in a gesture that took in the whole room as well as the frenzied group sex that was taking place on the far side. "I'm offering you a partnership in the chateau."

"That's an amazing offer, and if things were different I'd be only too happy to accept. But there's something I must deal with at home."

For a moment, Chantel's classically beautiful face clouded. Removing Ali's hand from where she'd held it, she let it drop. "You mean there's someone you must see."

With more conviction than she actually felt, Ali smiled. "Yes, someone."

She hadn't even admitted it to herself until now, but there was an emotional vacuum inside her and probably only one person who could go even half way to filling it. She'd always known it deep down, of course, but it wasn't the kind of thing you shouted about. How she wished for the gift of clairvoyance, longed to know whether the object of her desire would be receptive or would rebuff her. But it was impossible to gauge and she had no other choice than to find out the hard way.

"I leave first thing in the morning."

"Then at least let me give you a parting gift."

Chantel clapped her hands and immediately two leather-clad women emerged from a side door. Walking between them, naked with his hands tied in front of him, was as tasty a blond hulk as Ali had ever seen. Tall and muscular, his torso rippled with every step he took.

"Take him," Chantel urged quietly, "and enjoy him - you've earned him! If you tire of him or things don't work out as you plan, then by all means bring him back. But I warn you," she laid a firm hand on Ali's knee, "next time you won't get away so easily."

CHAPTER ONE

Ali settled herself in the chair, sinking into the luxury of the oversized seat cushion. At first she'd been concerned that the leopard print covering would appear tacky, but it turned out to be the perfect accessory for the wide, black wooden chair, as was the matching cushion against which she rested her back.

Resting her elbows over the wooden arms of the chair, she listened to Jurgen moving about in the bedroom. How long did it take him to make the bed, for goodness sake? All he had to do was smooth the sheet, fluff up the duck feather pillows and pull up the bloody quilt. A smile curved her lips and warmth flared in her belly as the memory came unbidden to her mind of the delicious way in which the bed had become so crumpled.

Last night, she'd allowed Jurgen to sleep with her, allowed him the hitherto unknown freedom to touch her as his own desire dictated. His strong hands had caressed her reverently at first, then more earnestly as his confidence increased. Lapsing into a blissful state and weakened by her own gnawing hunger to feel a cock inside her, she'd done nothing to prevent his throbbing penis from pounding frenziedly inside her, filling her with his scalding seed without as much as a plea for forgiveness.

Clearly she'd allowed him too much. It must never happen again if she were to retain her position of authority and command his respect.

Banishing the memory of how nice it had been to the back of her mind, she checked her watch, and was relieved to note that she didn't have to leave just yet. If her recollections of Leigh McFarlane were correct, she was always late. Ali doubted her friend had changed much over the half dozen years since they'd last met. The poor girl had always been a bit scatty, and had a tendency to be a bit of a stick-in-the-mud if the truth be told. If it hadn't been for Ali, Leigh would never have got round to doing half the things she'd done - including losing her virginity.

With a satisfied smile, Ali cast her eye over her new home. The whole place had an air of sophistication, and she knew she'd been lucky to acquire the spacious apartment at such short notice. Taking up the entire seventeenth floor, it was perfect for her current needs - in time she could also acquire the apartment downstairs.

Situated right in the heart of the Hertfordshire town, where the head offices of a corporate giant had once stood, Riverside Tower looked out over the shopping centre on two of its four sides, with fine views across the river, fields and down to the railway station on the third. On a clear day, you could just catch a glimpse of the canal from the fourth side.

The midday sun streamed in through the blinds, making the highly polished floorboards positively gleam. Ali allowed herself another smile, knowing that a barrel load of elbow grease had gone into the polishing, just as it had done on the rest of the black wood and smoked glass furniture.

Resting her feet on the glass topped coffee table, Ali crossed her legs at the ankles while she fiddled with her white, silk blouse. She wanted everything to look just so. Opening the top two buttons, she arranged the collar carefully over the lapels of her black jacket. Handmade by a top London tailor, the trouser suit fitted her perfectly, accentuating her womanly curves and narrow waist. She was a woman with oodles of sex appeal, and she knew it. Men lusted after her and that was just the way she liked it - it was merely a matter of controlling it.

Leaning back with her fingers linked behind her head, she felt the familiar stirrings in her belly, uncoiling like a spiral of erotic current that needed only a spark to cause an explosion. Damn Jurgen! There wasn't time to assuage her lust now, but at least she could lessen the desire and hold off the detonation until her return. Then she'd make him pay for his audacity.

"Jurgen. Stop what you're doing and come here. Now."

Within seconds, the brawny blond was scurrying towards her. Naked as always, his muscles rippled excitingly with controlled energy beneath his tanned skin. His limp phallus, though magnificent when erect, now hung like a deflated balloon between his thick thighs.

Without moving, she stared at him coolly as he came and stood before her.

"Yes, Mistress?"

"Cigar."

He had lovely buttocks, she thought as he scuttled away to retrieve one of the finest cigars that Cuba had to offer. She thrilled at how it felt to close her hands over the cheeks, how it felt to dig her fingers deep into the malleable flesh. Ah, when she came home...

Jurgen selected a cigar from the ebony box, and Ali felt a warm surge of power as she watched him trim the end, then place it between his lips. He was a non-smoker and she was fully aware of how much he hated this particular chore, but she was also aware of how much he feared not to do it. He held the silver lighter to the end, lit the cigar, coughed as he drew on it to make sure it was alight, then came back to her.

With long, chunky fingers, Jurgen placed the cigar between Ali's open red lips and she clamped it between her teeth. For the first time she wondered if he suspected the truth, that her distaste was almost as great as his own. But it was good for her image to be seen smoking a cigar, besides adding to her feeling of superiority. And she knew he hated that, the same way he hated the need within him to submit, even as he hungered to be controlled.

"Well, don't just stand there," she said without removing the cigar from the corner of her mouth. "Surely you don't expect me to go out with dirty shoes!"

Immediately, he dropped to his knees. He lifted her foot, encased in the black, spike-heeled shoe, as reverently as if it were some religious artefact. Slowly, he bowed his head. After working his lips together to try and increase his salvia, he poked out his long, pink tongue. Then, without a word of dissent, Jurgen proceeded to lick the already shining black shoe.

***

Leigh stole a glance beneath her lashes as she pushed down the waistband of her tight, black skirt, watching as Owen tugged at the knot of his tie. In his forties with swept back dark hair and conservative dress code, he looked every inch the respectable family doctor. So it had come as something of a surprise to his young receptionist that his pursuit of her had been quite so vigorous. But flattering though it was, it had taken away the fun of flashing her legs at an unavailable man.

"Do you need some help with that?" he asked lecherously as she wriggled the skirt over her hips.

"No," her giggle was that of a girl much younger than her twenty-four years, "I can manage, thank you, Doctor."

The formal way she addressed him was as mischievous as the way she turned sideways to rest her chin on her shoulder, looking back at him coquettishly from beneath long lashes. There was a mischievous look about her voluminous hair, too, the red-gold tousled curls giving her the sensuous look of someone who'd just stepped out of bed. Of course, the look often took hours to achieve, but the effect was quite devastating.

Letting her skirt drop to the floor, she stepped out of it as elegantly as she was able before holding it up triumphantly between finger and thumb. "Ta-da!"

"Yes, very good." The little cock teaser wasn't wearing any knickers! Laughing, he shrugged out of his grey suit and crisp, white shirt and watched her slowly unfasten the buttons of her blouse. She was like a teenager flirting with the boys - the little bitch knew it turned him on.

"You'll be the death of me, young lady, especially if my wife finds out."

"How could she?" Leigh felt the current that always buzzed through her at times like this. She loved to see men want her, eyeing her up and slowly succumbing to her teasing. Sometimes she'd give in to them, sometimes she wouldn't. She didn't mean anything by it, it was just a bit of fun. And boy! Was she having fun with the good Doctor Brand.

Her fingers swirled over the soft, white flesh of her inner thigh, between the top of her black hold-ups and her furry red mound.

Owen swallowed. "I'm supposed to be meeting her after morning surgery, and the last patient left over fifteen minutes ago."

With her fingers fumbling between her shoulder blades, Leigh unhooked her lacy, white bra. "Oh! That reminds me. I'm meeting someone for lunch, too."

"Anyone I should know about? A jealous boyfriend, perhaps? Get a move on, Sweetheart. Jump up on the couch or we'll both be late."

"An old school friend," Leigh swayed her hips provocatively as she crossed the small room, "who's been living abroad."

Standing now with her mons pressed against the edge of the examination couch and her hands resting on top, she presented him with her pert backside as she made a show of hoisting herself up. With her heart racketing madly in her ribcage, she leaned forward with her weight on her hands and lifted her right knee, clambering up like a child climbing onto a forbidden wall. Then, pulling her other leg up, on all fours she turned around so that her head faced the pillow end.

The couch springs protested loudly under the added weight of Owen. Also on all fours as he settled himself behind her, he held her trim waist as he positioned himself more comfortably. Then, with his erect cock nestling in the deep crevice between the lovely cheeks of her bottom, he reached forward to take her breasts in his palms.

"Oh Owen."

Her words were little more than a sigh as his hands closed tightly around her firm globes, kneading them gently at first before giving them a squeeze. Then, still holding them tightly, his fingers and thumbs found her nipples. And as he rolled and tweaked them, so they hardened and swelled.

The throbbing of her nipples sent a warm tingling throughout her insides, finally setting up a mirrored throbbing in her clitoris. And as he moved his penis back and forth along her tight crevice, she wasn't sure if it was the thrill of the act itself or the thought of getting caught that excited her more.

Relinquishing his hold on her right breast, his fingers closed around his shaft and he guided it between her open legs. Then, as the purple head of his cock began to nudge at the engorged lips of her labia, she knew - it was the thrill of being caught!

Using two fingers, he parted her labia like a flower and pushed his way in, past her inner lips into the warm, moist depths of her vagina until his shaft was buried up to the hilt. And then he thrust, and thrust again, building up a rhythm as she ground her buttocks against him.

Sighing and panting, their groans of pleasure mingled, building up to a crescendo of noise that echoed in the small room. Her muscles contracted tightly around his flesh as he neared his point of no return. And then, with a growl from deep in his throat, he emptied the scalding contents of his balls inside her quivering, convulsing sex as every muscle in her body locked rigid.

***

During Ali's absence, The Rose and Crown had become The Town Crier. No longer the convivial, everyone's favourite 'local' in the town centre, now it was a themed pub, cashing in on the town's long history. Where the laughing, bustling hordes had once gathered, now the punters were all office workers - not a builder, shop worker or car mechanic in sight. The conversations revolved around office politics and new computer systems rather than the changing fortunes of the local football team and who did what to whom last Friday.

The refit was all very well done, Ali thought as she looked around at the pseudo relics, paintings and life-sized wooden effigies of local celebrities throughout the ages, but the place was sadly lacking in atmosphere. She cast a critical eye over the effigy that stood beside the bar, and so didn't see the landlord leave a large group of late arrivals to serve her.

"Haven't seen you in here before. New recruit at Blestows?"

Ali turned her attention to the landlord, a middle-aged man with a middle-aged spread and pebble-dash face.

"That's Braddock," he supplied helpfully, without giving her time to answer and nodding towards the effigy, "one of the last Highwaymen to be hanged in the country. Over there," he said, pointing to another life-sized representation, "is Maitland, the old Magistrate who sentenced him. Everyone knew he was in cahoots with Braddock, and only had him hung to save his own neck. No one's ever found the booty."

Ali, whose own roots went back as far as the town's, was unimpressed to see her illustrious ancestor so publicly ridiculed.

"Brandy," she stated flatly. Turning her back on the landlord, she began walking, calling out over her shoulder, "I'll be sitting over there."

"Hey! I'm not here to wait on tables."

"You are now."

From her corner table by the window, Ali would be able to see Leigh's arrival, as well as keeping an eye on the other punters. She also had a good view of Magistrate Maitland, from whom she'd inherited the sadistic streak, but sadly not the family fortune. That was long gone.

"Your drink." The brandy splashed over the side as the landlord plonked the glass down. Standing slightly behind her, he made no move to return to his work.

"You've spilt it."

"Sorry!" he said, sarcastically.

"You will be."

Lifting her glass with her left hand, surreptitiously, she reached out her right behind her. He was wearing thin cotton trousers. All the better! Her long fingers began feeling up the inside of his leg, sending spirals of quivering warmth from her tight breasts to her pussy as she imagined the electrifying effect it was having on him.

With that, her hand closed tightly and viciously around his semi-hard penis. She smiled as she heard the grunt of pain as he tried to stop himself from yelling out. With a satisfied smile, she took a swig from her glass before replacing it on the table. And as she did so, she squeezed again, but this time, without releasing her hold.

"Your name is?" she prompted.

"John. John Micklem."

"Well, John Micklem, Thursday evening, come to Riverside Tower at nine o'clock. It's only across the road from here. "

"I can't. I'm working."

"No, you're not. You'll wait in the lobby until I send for you. I won't stand for unpunctuality. It goes without saying that you'll come alone and won't tell anyone." She gave another sharp squeeze that had him crying out aloud, causing several heads to turn towards the sound. "I trust I make myself clear."

"Yes."

She released her hold. "Now get back to work."

Under the gaze of a group of customers, and without a backward glance, John made for the bar.

Her distinctive, unruffled silk tones followed him. "Oh, John!"

He stopped in his tracks.

"That's an awfully small willy you've got!"

Lifting her glass to her lips, she could feel the acuteness of his embarrassment as the whole place erupted in laughter. Watching as he scuttled off through a doorway that led to the kitchen, Ali felt the familiar, glorious, high-intensity volts of arousal that shook her insides.

***

"Get out, you stupid little bitch! What are you waiting for, money?"

"Money?" Leigh's head shot up, indignation rising like bile in her stomach. "How dare you! What do you take me for, a common whore?"

"Then what? Do you think you've got some kind of hold over me?" he hissed poison-edged words across the room.

Too amazed to deny his insane accusations, her soft mouth fell open. The man was cracking up! With the resentful pain of denial in her eyes, she watched as his hand shook with rage.

"Surely you're not one of those girls that thinks one quick fuck constitutes love. If so, you can put that idea right out of your head. In case it's escaped your notice, I'm already married, and have no intention of leaving my wife for a slip of a girl."

"But Owen-"

"Listen, young lady. You breathe one word of this to anyone," hastily pulling on his trousers, Owen tugged angrily at the metal hasp of the zip, "and you'll be out on your ear. I'll put the word around amongst my colleagues that you're a troublemaker. I'll tell them how you can't be trusted, that the confidentiality of patients is in jeopardy with you on the premises. I'll make sure that you never work as a doctor's receptionist again." He gave the hasp another tug. Damn! His bloody flies were jammed. How the hell could he meet Nina like this?

Still naked on the couch, Leigh shivered. Her staring, wide eyes reflected her astonishment. What on earth had got into the man? He'd changed from an intelligent, though spineless, middle-aged individual who couldn't keep his cock in his pants to an objectionable, blackmailing lunatic.

All at once she felt dirty and abused... and way out of her depth. Anxiety stirred in the depths of her bowels. God, what would she do if he carried out his threat? She couldn't afford to lose this job.

Torn between defiance and flight, she realised the latter was out of the question since she still had no clothes on. So she could either tell him where he could stick his job or swallow her pride and beg him to reconsider. After all, she could always continue to work here while looking for another job elsewhere.

Deciding that the second idea was the best option, she opened her mouth to speak. But she heard herself with growing disquiet, as heated indignation made her reckless and the words came out all wrong.

"That's some wild ego trip you're on! Look, Doctor Brand," she emphasised his name as acidly as she was able, "of course I won't tell anyone. It wasn't that good. Ok, it was fun, but as far as I'm concerned, it was a one-off. I'm not in the slightest bit interested in a relationship, with you or anyone else. I like my life just as it is, thank you very much." She swung her long, shapely legs off the couch and stooped to retrieve her clothes from the floor. "You get on with your life and I'll get on with mine. As far as I'm concerned, this little bit of... hanky-bloody-panky never happened."

Straightening up, she caught his bitterly hostile eye, and knew she'd gone too far. His long, lean face turned crimson as his anger increased. He was visibly shaking as he strode towards her, every step full of menace. Snatching up his stethoscope from his desk as he passed, he bunched it up in his hand.

A blaze of pain erupted across her cheek as he swung the instrument and made contact with her pale face. No one had ever hit her before and she cried out, more in astonishment than pain. Her hand cupped her cheek as if that could soothe the fire, and the sudden, unexplained tightness of her breasts.

"On the contrary. If you want to keep your job," his tone suggested she was a wayward child in need of a good thrashing, "you'll be available as and when I decide. I'm not interested if the earth moves for you or not. My only concerns are that you keep that pretty little mouth of yours shut and your adorable pussy open. Do I make myself clear?"

Leigh trembled as he raised his hand a second time. She'd heard about men like him, weirdoes that got off on intimidation and violence. Slowly, she nodded her head. Even as she agreed to become his unpaid whore, she made herself a solemn vow; she didn't know when or how, but she'd pay him back. How did the saying go? Something about not getting sore but getting even?

CHAPTER TWO

"Here." Ali handed Leigh the glass of wine before she was even seated. "You look done in. Something wrong?"

"No," Leigh lied as she took the seat opposite her friend.

Lifting the glass to her lips, Leigh took a sip of the dry house white they served there, then smiled fleetingly to mask her shock at the change in her old friend's appearance. Everything was different, not only the way she wore her hair, but also her taste in clothes. Even her make-up was more brazen than it used to be, though in all honesty, Ali had never gone in for subtlety.

For some reason that she couldn't fathom, Leigh felt strange prickles of discomfort in the company of the woman who had once been her dearest friend. She'd imagined this scene often over the past weeks; the hugs and kisses, the wild excitement, the joyful tears. Yet all she could manage now was a flustered, "Hey, it's good to see you after all this time. You look... great!"

Ali had already picked up the warning signals from Leigh's body language, and now she became aware of the distress flares in her voice. While it was clear that something other than Ali's changed appearance was bothering Leigh, Ali didn't want to add to her distress and frighten her off. There would be plenty of time later for Ali to exert her authority over the pretty redhead, but for now, she must take things at a more leisurely pace.

Deciding on a light-hearted tone for their first meeting, Ali forced a little laugh.

"Your legs seem even longer than I remember, but you're not as bubbly as you used to be. Are you always this miserable or is it just seeing me again?"

"Oh, bad day at the office," Leigh quipped, trying to match Ali's easygoing manner, though even to her own ears her usually animated voice sounded leaden, "you know how it is."

"No, I don't."

There was an awkward silence, during which Ali swept her dark, rapacious eyes over Leigh's curvy stature, and felt the familiar stirrings of arousal warming her loins.

Physically, Leigh had blossomed. No longer the willowy, small breasted teenager that Ali had left behind, Leigh had grown into a very sexy lady indeed, with a figure Ali herself would die for. Her breasts had developed into two lavishly firm globes, if the way they strained against her white blouse was anything to go by, and served to accentuate her slim waist. Her slightly rounded belly and curvaceous hips tapered to long, shapely legs. And her pretty, red-gold hair shone with a hectic brilliance.

But whatever it was that was bothering Leigh, its effect on her face was devastating. She looked weary and her normally pale skin seemed bleached of colour, and wasn't helped by her understated make-up. Her grey-green eyes seemed to have lost their mischievous lustre and the coquettish pout of her lips was uncharacteristically sullen.

This wasn't the joyful homecoming Ali had imagined. The pain of Leigh's cold-shoulder would have struck at the very heart of her, were it not for her own obstinacy. Determined to get to the root of the trouble, she slapped a smile across her lips and put all her energy into her laid-back jokiness as she probed gently.

"Come on, Leigh, spill the beans. Where are you working?"

"I'm a receptionist at the Doctor's surgery in Grovedale Road."

Ali grinned mischievously. "Doctors, eh? Horny devils. Receptionist my eye! I bet they have you running around in a sexy little nurse's outfit."

Relieved that her friend's humour hadn't changed as much as her appearance, Ali's joviality nevertheless grated on Leigh's nerves. She knew she was being cranky, but that business with Owen had really got to her. Thank God she had the rest of the day off; she didn't think she could have faced him at evening surgery.

Longing for the close relationship of the old days when they'd been more like sisters than friends, Leigh longed to unburden herself, confide her troubles to Ali. But somehow she didn't feel totally at ease in her company, and besides, it hardly seemed fair to lay it all at Ali's feet when the poor woman had only just arrived home.

***

Ali swigged back the last of her brandy, then holding the empty glass aloft; she clicked her fingers in the air.

Embarrassed by her friend's brash behaviour, Leigh's eyes flicked nervously from Ali to the bar and back again.

"You've been away too long! I don't know what kind of places you've been spending your time in, but this is a pub, not a restaurant. You can't expect them to wait on you when they've so many other customers to serve."

"No?" Ali raised her eyebrows in an expression of feigned surprise. "Watch and learn."

Without turning her head to look in his direction as John hurried to her side, tersely Ali ordered another brandy for herself and a second wine for Leigh.

"Ali!" Leigh hissed as John scuttled off, and then gave a little laugh before adding with a hint of respect, "you could at least have said 'please'!"

When John returned with the drinks, Ali leaned back in her chair. Under Leigh's shocked but oh-so-admiring gaze, Ali partly veiled her eyes with her long black lashes and gazed flirtingly at John. She flicked out her tongue and licked her lips in a way that was clearly meant to be provocative.

As he turned to go, Ali said, "I haven't dismissed you yet." Power was a definite turn on and once again she felt a warm, erotic thrill. The arousal in her loins spread to her breasts; her nipples hardened and throbbed. She closed her thighs tightly as if that could ease the aching of her moistening sex. "If you were a dog, you'd sit at my feet. I want you to remember that, John. Bring a collar and lead with you on Thursday. If you're a good boy, I'll give you a treat. If not..." Ali smiled a crocodile smile, "I'll punish you. Now, go away. My friend and I have some unfinished business."

Leigh's face was a picture, a mix of incredulity and adoration- with just a smidgen of unease in her eyes. There was real command in Ali's harsh tone, and a hunger that was just as real in the landlord's eyes. She watched in amazement as dutifully, he returned to the bar.

"Ali! You're outrageous!" Leigh's giggle was the soft, tinkling sound that Ali remembered. "What was all that about?"

"Nothing you need concern yourself with just yet." Ali took a swig from her glass and tried to clamp down the erotic charges that pulsed through her. "So, is there anyone special in your life, Leigh?"

"No." The question touched a raw nerve, and immediately, the brief sense of fun drained from Leigh's pale face. Her shoulders slumped dejectedly.

"Hey, what's with the mood swings?" Ali waited until Leigh lifted her eyes to meet hers. "Lighten up." She raised her hands in an impatient gesture. "It's like trying to get blood out of the proverbial stone with you. After my being away for so long, I thought it would be fun to catch up. But if this is the best you can do, then perhaps I should just turn around and head back the way I came."

Leigh held the suddenly hostile gaze from Ali's dark, heavily made-up, kohl lined eyes and felt a sudden surge of guilt. What right had she to judge Ali's behaviour when her own bordered on rudeness?

"I'm sorry, Ali. It really is great to see you, but I've had a rough morning. No, there's no one special. To be honest, I've got a bit of a downer with men at the moment. As far as I'm concerned, the world would be a better place without them!"

Sucking in the air between her teeth, Ali joked. "Surely you haven't gone off sex, Leigh? Here I am, dying for a bit of dirty gossip with my best friend, and you sit there all po-faced. I know you've never been the type to brag, but you must have something to tell."

Leigh sipped her drink and placed the glass on the table with as much care as she employed to assemble her thoughts. Although they'd once been great friends, always in each other's company, Leigh had never been in the same league as Ali. Great fun to be with, Ali had always been the life and soul of any gathering, and at first, Leigh had found life dull without her. But slowly, Leigh had built a new life for herself and wasn't at all sure if there was room in it now for Ali.

In a last ditch attempt to salvage what was left of their time together, Leigh announced suddenly, "you've changed. What happened to those gorgeous long, wavy black locks? It's not that the short, swept back look doesn't suit you," she cast a critical eye over Ali's shiny, slicked back style, "it's just that it's going to take an awful lot of getting used to. And the suit..."

"You don't like it?"

"Yes." Anxious not to offend, Leigh gabbled, "Yes, of course. But it makes you look kind of... I don't know... sort of intimidating, especially with your hair like that. Let's put it this way..." relaxing at last, Leigh giggled, "I wouldn't want to argue with you!"

Now both girls laughed as the memories of their sometimes volatile friendship came flooding back. It wasn't that she hadn't had a mind of her own, Leigh acknowledged now, it was just that Ali had always been the natural leader. Right from that very first meeting in secondary school, Leigh had found it hard to resist Ali's more forceful temperament. Though she'd often fought hard against it, sometimes even resorting to shouting and screaming her defiance at her best friend, she had always given in eventually. It had seemed as natural as breathing to yield in the end, to comply with whatever her friend suggested, more often than not landing herself in a whole heap of trouble.

Now, leaning with her elbows on the table, Leigh lifted her drink to her lips. Lowering her eyes, her tone grew more serious as she risked the question that had haunted her for years.

"Why did you take off like that? Your parents - everyone was worried sick. There was a nation-wide hunt for you. As far as I'm aware, you're still officially listed as a missing person."

"No," Ali reached out and covered her friend's hand with her own, "I'm not. The hunt was called off when I made contact with the police. They, of course, insisted on putting me in touch with my relatives. We spoke briefly on the phone, and I told them of my decision to travel across Europe." Ali thought back over her recent past and smiled. "I had no intention of falling in with everyone's plans for me. I told them that I was never coming back."

"So why did you?"

"I made enquiries. I discovered that my folks had moved away, but you hadn't. So, here I am." Leaning forward, Ali ran the back of her finger up Leigh's arm. "Oh, Leigh, I've got so much to tell you, so much I want to teach you."

Leigh had never been touched so seductively by another woman, and to her dismay, she rather liked it- in an uncomfortable sort of way, of course. She felt discomfort between her thighs and tried to disguise the fact by shifting in her seat. To add to her troubles, Ali's lips curved into a knowing smile.

Fidgeting relentlessly now as she drained her glass, Leigh plonked it down on the table. Strange flutters in her stomach unsettled her further and she withdrew her arm from Ali's reach.

Ali's voice was soft and compelling when she spoke.

"I bet that pussy of your is twitching. Why don't you give it what it wants?"

"Pardon? Did I hear you right?"

"Go on, Leigh, give it what it wants. Play with yourself."

"What, here? Don't be stupid." Leigh coloured up at the suggestion and giggled nervously. "I can't! The landlord's probably already got it in for us after the things you said. He'll throw me out if he catches me."

Ali flicked her eyes across to the bar, where John was standing with one arm resting on the bar, his eyes fixed on the two girls.

"No, he won't. Go on, Leigh. You know you want to. Just slip your finger inside your vagina."

"People will see!" Even as she protested, Leigh's shaky hand delved beneath the hem of her skirt and nudged between her hot thighs.

"So what? Don't you like to be watched?"

Unable to answer for the erratic pulse that had taken up residence in her throat, Leigh drew in a ragged breath. Thankful that she wasn't wearing panties, she worked her finger between the hot folds of her already moist sex. Nervously, she reached for her empty glass with her free hand, trying to steady herself by gripping the stem tightly, while the finger of her other hand slid in and out of her ever moistening pussy. Slowly, in and out, and again, in and out.

"Faster, Leigh," Ali instructed, her smile radiant and her eyes shining with her own lust, "faster."

Even as Leigh imagined the outrage of other customers, even as her face turned crimson, her dextrous finger built up speed.

"Don't forget your clitoris," Ali instructed softly, "use your thumb."

As her finger continued its agitation of her sweet opening, Leigh's thumb sought out her hard, throbbing bud. Spirals of exhilaration warmed her insides, setting off all kinds of tingles and twitches as her excitement increased. She knew it was wrong, but it was oh so exciting to play with herself like this, here, in public with her best friend watching.

"There, that's so good," Ali whispered silkily, "you'll be coming soon. A little more, faster, faster. Are you coming?"

Leigh bit into her lip and closed her eyes in an effort to hold back the unstoppable cramps. The muscles of her sex clamped tightly around her finger, while every other muscle in her body tensed. She mustn't come, not here. But oh! Let her come now!

She threw back her head. And, under the scandalized gaze of the dwindling band of lunchtime customers, Leigh's orgasm hit with an impact that ripped a muffled cry from her throat.

***

Jurgen fell to his knees. He raised his eyes, pleadingly, as a dog does when watching his owner tuck into a juicy steak.

Ali stood before him, a formidable woman in a black Basque. Wearing nothing else save her spike-heeled shoes and an exquisite choker of beaded jet, as always, her make-up was as bold as her nature. The shape of her black eyebrows was emphasised at the nose end with pencil, making them appear thicker and giving her a sterner expression. Lined in kohl, her dark eyes, like glittering nuggets of coal, were further emphasised by eye shadow. Not soft, smoky browns or cool blues and mauves, no, Ali preferred more vibrant tones like the deep turquoise she wore today. And her glossed lips were scarlet.

Quivering with anticipation, Jurgen held up his hand as if in prayer, linking his strong fingers. Lifting her leg to rest her foot on Jurgen's broad, bare shoulder, without a word, Ali bound his wrists together. She used her preferred cord, similar to that of curtain tie backs. Tying it tightly, she watched him grimace as it bit into his flesh.

CHAPTER THREE

A li's cruelty continued over the next few days. Now, the cold, stainless steel metal bars, each with a four inch girth, dug into Jurgen's back. Alone in the darkness, he was spread-eagled against them, his legs stretched wide and his ankles tied by biting cord to the bottom bar. His wrists were also tied, stretched wide and attached above his head. And to make matters worse, his thighs and back had been cruelly marked with angry looking criss-cross weals from Ali's thin cane. Bruising already stained his abdomen, testifying to the viciousness of Ali's small fists.

The pain was agonizing, every breath bringing new waves of rawness, as if someone had kicked him repeatedly from the inside.

Ali, or 'Mistress Blackheart' as she called herself, had left the apartment several hours ago without as much as a goodbye, nor even a mention of when he could expect her home. Not that he'd any right to expect such pleasantries, since she was the mistress and he merely the slave. He hung his head despondently.

The bitch had done this room out as what she called 'the playroom' with all kinds of apparatus, including the wall bars to which he was now secured. Reaching from floor to ceiling with about six inches between them, they took up the entire expanse of one stark, white wall.

Even the floorboards were glaringly white.

A flood of humiliation swept over him as Jurgen wondered just what kind of madness kept him from fighting back. Where was the pride, the willpower that had driven him to lift weights during his youth, enabling him to throw off the 'weakling' tag of his early years to become a perfect specimen of manhood.

With a chest as hard as a brick wall and pectorals as big as houses, dignity should be his watchword, not humiliation. As a former holder of the Master of the Globe title, his strength was many times superior to Ali's; he could easily overpower her, even with one hand tied behind his back and his legs fettered.

So how was it he was tethered here, like a bull in a stall? If only he could repress the whorls of fevered lust that created the need within him - the need to be utterly dominated by beautiful women.

His head jerked up as the door crashed open. He screwed up his eyes against the harsh light that flooded the white room, bounced off the stainless steel wall bars and wall racks and threw the black frames of the other apparatus into stark contrast.

The door banged shut again with a dreadful finality. When his eyes finally adjusted to the light he saw Ali standing just inside the door, her right hand resting on the swell of her hip and a cigar in her left hand.

"Look at you! Call yourself a man? I've seen better specimens than you in bottles."

His eyes raked the length of her exquisite, small boned body. What a sight she was! Again wearing the choker, instead of shoes she wore black leather, thigh-hugging boots, with spiked heels of at least four inches. The Basque was different, too, made of black leather with peepholes that allowed her stiff, dark brown nipples to poke through. She wasn't wearing panties and he gulped at the sight of the thatch of wiry hair between her thighs and her fleshy, elongated labia, invitingly open and warm.

"You disgust me!" She opened her legs, a little at first, then wider, then wider still. "I'm the hardest bitch you'll ever kneel before and you will obey me, even if

I have to bind that pathetic little worm between your legs to your balls. What do you say, Jurgen?"

"Yes, Mistress."

"But you'd probably like that, wouldn't you, slave?"

"Yes, Mistress."

She took a drag on her cigar. Her nipples stood out like bullets from her upward tilting breasts, and there was a tell-tale trickle making its lazy way down the inside of her thigh.

"You've let me down again- you didn't prepare my evening meal. It's not bloody good enough! If you don't buck up your ideas, I'll replace you. Do you understand, wimp?"

Jurgen drew in a long breath. Anger rose at the back of his head and settled over his knitted brows, just as surely as heat rose in his balls. How the hell was he supposed to prepare a meal when the bitch didn't allow him out to buy groceries? He could hardly cook when he was tied in here for hours on end!

"Well? I'm waiting. Do you want me to replace you?"

"No, Mistress."

"Then don't cock up again. From now on, you'll order everything from the supermarket, online!"

Just seeing him so helpless made her pulses throb excitedly. To have any man under her control was thrilling, but to have a man as impressively built as Jurgen made the blood dance in her veins and heat flare in her loins. Crazy with the power that flowed through her, her hand slipped from her hip to her sex. She toyed with her pulsating clitoris as she took another drag on her cigar, in an effort to stop her hand from shaking.

"I'd have gone fucking hungry if it hadn't been for some businessman I met at the Royal Barge Hotel, who had the good grace to ask me to join him at his table after we'd fucked."

Her eyes raked his tethered body with a look that suggested Jurgen was less than half the man of her mysterious dinner companion, and the derisory tone with which she delivered her speech triggered the feral urges that clutched at her insides. She wanted him- but more than that, she wanted to make him suffer, merely for suffering's sake. It gave her a tremendous thrill to know that she really was a black hearted bitch.

"I went back to his room afterwards for a quickie." She narrowed her eyes and almost smiled. "What else could I do, since he was so generous with the Dom Perignon? God! He was so well hung!" She paused to give Jurgen's magnificent, stirring cock a hungry look, then added sneeringly, "not like that basket of withered fruit that you're so proud of."

Helpless in his bonds, he watched as the bitch rubbed her clitoris. He wanted her so much, he was going crazy; his balls were on fire. He struggled to wrench himself free. His blood pumped wildly, making his cock twitch into semi-hardness. The heart that beat in his massive chest took up a frantic thumping, sending echoes to his pulses that joined in the mad rhythm. He couldn't stop the low growl that escaped from his throat.

"So," she eyed his stiffening phallus with a scornful glance, "you still want me." She took a long drag on her cigar, then blew out the acrid smoke through sneering lips and watched it curl towards the ceiling.

The beating of her own heart quickened as she strutted towards him. Her blood swept like lava through her veins as her excitement mounted. She loved the thrill of power that made her insides quake, and knew she'd have to find relief somehow. But she wasn't about to give Jurgen what he wanted just yet. No, let him wait! After all, she was never without a vibrator close at hand. And that pretty little blonde was due to arrive soon...

Coming to a halt in front of him, she gyrated her hips lewdly as her finger slipped inside the warmth of her moist vagina. Again she took a drag from her cigar, stared unblinkingly into his eyes, and then blew the smoke directly in his face.

A sanguine smile lit up her face and her eyes sparkled like the jet of her choker as he began to cough.

"Poor Jurgen. He really doesn't like cigars," she said flicking the ash on his right shoulder, "does he?" She wet her lips with her tongue. The heady mix of sexual agitation and cold superiority threatened to engulf her; she must relieve herself soon, or submit to the hungry cock that reared upward from his groin.

No way! She was Mistress here - she'd decide when and where they'd fuck.

Slowly, she withdrew her honey-wreathed fingers and wiped them dismissively on his left shoulder at the same time as she stubbed out the cigar on his right. There was the slightest hint of burning flesh in the air as his body tensed.

Her thin smile was cruel. The veins in her swanlike neck grew more prominent as she threw back her head, laughing joyously at the contorted look on Jurgen's face as he tried to bite back a bitter retort.

"No," she scoffed, straightening up, "you wouldn't dare answer me back, you snivelling piece of shit."

Without warning, she dealt his iron cock a stinging blow, so viciously that she sent it arcing down to thump the top of his groin before springing upright again. She loved the way it seemed to swell even more.

"You want to fuck me, don't you?"

His words came out as a strangled, "yes, Mistress."

"I didn't hear you", she snarled, then delivered a resounding slap to his face, which brought her immediate gratification in the form of an instant red glow across his tanned cheek. He was close to coming, and she'd have to time it well if she were to leave the room before that happened. "Tell me what you want."

"I want to fuck you, Mistress Blackheart."

"Tough! It's getting late, and I'm expecting a visitor, a sweet little nymphet by the name of Cindy. You'll have to make do with listening at the keyhole." She laughed, then said as if it were an afterthought, "oh, but you can't! You're a little tied up at the moment. It will be an hour or so before I get time to release you."

She sashayed back across the room, swaying her hips provocatively. She could hear him straining at his bonds, hear his grunts and groans as he tried to hold back the inevitable.

Turning briefly, she said, "incidentally, I brought you back a doggie bag from the hotel - you'll find half a bread roll and a small piece of Brie. Since you're unable to eat it just yet, I'll leave it in the kitchen and you can have it for breakfast while you're preparing mine."

There was a wild, animal cry from deep in his throat as he tugged frenziedly at his bonds as she reached the door. The sound of thick liquid hitting the floor brought a cold smile to her lips as she flicked off the light.

***

Leigh couldn't sleep. She lay beside her sleeping lover, churning the events of the last few days over in her mind while twirling her hardened nipples between finger and thumb. Inevitably, her mind drifted to her meeting with Ali, and her friend's outrageous behaviour. What in Heaven's name had possessed her to speak to John Micklem like that?

Leigh had been in that particular pub several times before, and had never considered the landlord to be a wimp- she allowed herself a secret smile- nor had her own mother.

Why hadn't he stood up to Ali? Except Leigh hadn't exactly stood up to Ali herself. Always bossy and a bit impertinent, the other day Ali had been nothing less than an arrogant, domineering bitch! Oh, the fun had still been there, but spread so thinly that it was barely there at all, other than as a disguise for something more sinister.

With her thigh resting against the warmth of Errol's, Leigh sighed heavily. Even twirling her cherry-like nipples hadn't relieved the sexual tension that had been building up inside her all day, gnawing at her insides like a hungry animal. It had started this morning, when Owen had again summoned her to his consulting room. As before, she'd enjoyed teasing him, but his performance hadn't lived up to expectations. She was sick of his continued threats! And he'd hit her again.

Deciding it was time to assuage her wantonness, she squirmed around in the bed to adjust her position. Then, sticking her bottom in the air, she dived beneath the bedclothes. Blindly crawling down toward the foot of the bed, barely able to breathe, she found Errol's foot and flicked out her tongue. As it darted between his toes, the tip of her warm, lascivious tongue brought sleepy grunts of approval to his lips as he woke up slowly.

Errol Proudfoot was the youngest of the three doctors in the practice, and mouth-wateringly handsome to boot! He was also the only one unmarried and she thought she probably loved him, though somehow his very eligibility dulled her excitement. Anyway, he wanted to keep their relationship quiet for the time being, because he was concerned that the other two doctors would think his behaviour with the young receptionist unprofessional. How little they knew!

Adjusting her position once more, she took the whole of his big toe into the warm cavern of her mouth, sucking it as diligently as if it were his magnificent organ.

"Oh, Baby," the way he whispered the word made it sound long, drawn out and extremely sexy, "you know how to please me."

Yes, she knew how to please him, to give him what he wanted. It was only her own needs that confused her. She knew she was an incorrigible flirt, a trait she'd picked up from Ali back in their teens, but these days she found the teasing more exciting than the sex itself. Surely it couldn't be right to always feel so let down after sex? It wasn't that she didn't orgasm - she did, often. It was just, well, her toes never curled and there were never any fireworks in her head.

She always got a thrill at the thought of being caught though, and it was high on her list of favourite things. Even while Owen was pumping into her this morning, she'd longed for the door to open and one of the other Doctors to come in and catch them. She suppressed a giggle as she sucked on Errol's toe- what if it had been Errol himself who'd caught them?

Oh, the sheer joy of fucking in public places! The local park on a sunny day, along the canal towpath, or even the supermarket car park. Once, she'd even done it in a graveyard. Come to think of it, that was when Ali had set her up - the Easter weekend when she'd lost her cherry to a boy from the visiting fair.

The memory sent a spiralling tingle from her breasts to her pussy. Releasing Errol's toe, she skittered her tongue over his satin skin, the colour of black grapes, and left a little trail of saliva as she worked up his leg with slow, sensual flicks. Swirling her tongue in tiny circling movements across his inner thigh, she felt the warmth from his crotch radiate across her face. Skimming her tongue upward, she flicked it in tiny darting movements across his balls, making him groan with pleasure.

Leigh thought again about Owen, how it had all gone pear shaped; how he was blackmailing her to keep her silence. Who the hell did he think he was? But she'd make him pay - there was no way she'd let him off after hitting her again - no had ever hit her.

Yet something was nagging at the back of her mind... something warm and erotic that she couldn't quite fathom.

She took Errol's glans between her lips, letting her tongue loiter at the ridge at the base of it. He made little noises deep in his throat as her sensually flicking tongue stimulated the highly sensitive area.

"Suck me, baby," he croaked between ragged breaths, "suck me."

She opened her mouth wide and took in the whole length of his impressive shaft. Little tremors passed from her breasts to her clitoris as she felt his cock pulsate deep in her throat. But something was wrong, nagging annoyingly at the back of her mind.

In a flash of revelation she knew what it was. When her flesh had warmed with the sting from Owen's hand, the feeling hadn't been wholly unpleasant; in a way, it had been kind of... well, weird... exciting, she supposed.

God! Surely it wasn't possible to enjoy pain! That was wrong, perverted - wasn't it? She felt herself tremble. It had to be wrong! Well, no one would ever strike her again and get away with it! She felt sick to the stomach - and unbelievably excited.

She grabbed the base of Errol's shaft and pulled it out of her mouth. Straightening up, she hauled herself up his gorgeous black, shiny body. Once she was in position she held open her thick, puffy labia with her tapered fingers.

She lowered herself over his smooth-skinned, iron erection, and her hungry sex sucked in his impressive phallus as if it were the first time she'd experienced the thrill. Excitedly, she built up a rhythm as she raised and lowered herself, bringing herself right to the edge of climax.

Errol's words caught huskily in his throat. "I'm coming, baby!"

His body jerked violently and he yelled as if his team had scored a goal as he shot jet after hot, powerful jet of semen into her tight channel.

For Leigh it was over too soon, and less than half a heartbeat later he'd pulled out of her. With a mumble that could have been gratitude, he turned over and went to sleep.

Rolling resignedly onto her back, Leigh's furious fingers sought out the hard bud of her clitoris. Hot with fevered need, she rubbed it briskly, trying to bring herself to the elusive climax. That made her think of how she'd brought herself to orgasm in the pub, under Ali's scrutiny.

Leigh's muscles tensed. As the tremors of orgasm ripped through her, one word breathed on a sigh escaped from her parted lips. "Ali..."

And in the soft, dreamy afterglow of orgasm, she wondered what her friend was doing tonight.

CHAPTER FOUR

It was well after midnight when, with a curt, "thank you" to the chauffeur who delivered the young girl, Ali closed the door. Excited to have what was in effect raw material to work with, without a word of greeting or pretence of kindness, she conducted the petite blonde through to the sitting room.

The young girl belonged to one of the most lecherous individuals in the whole of southern England. But then, as Ali understood it, he'd not had her for long and had acquired her 'sight unseen.' Ali smiled a thin smile - the guy would be in for quite a treat by the time she'd finished with her.

At under five feet, the girl tottered about on high, purple stilettos which made her appear taller. Given that this was the first time she'd ever worn them, the ungainly swing it gave to her narrow hips was only to be expected - and would be corrected under Ali's guidance.

Blessed, or perhaps cursed by her own sexuality, Ali enjoyed the delights to be obtained from males and females alike, the only conditions being that it was she who did the ravishing, she who remained in control. And now, as she brought the girl to a halt in the sitting room, Ali was drawn to the youngster's alluring innocence.

"Strip!"

"Sorry?" Stunned by the command as well as Ali's stern appearance, her attention wavered, coming to rest on Ali's hard, dark nipples which poked through her Basque. The girl's shy, nervous gaze flicked downward to Ali's naked lower regions, where elongated pussy lips were visible beneath the thick, black wiry pubes.

The girl dared a question. "What did you say?"

"I said 'strip!' you stupid little tart!" Ali tapped a long-handled whip against the side of her leather-encased thigh. The twelve, narrow, leather fronds danced malevolently around the ankles of her high, leather boots. "You know why you're here, so get on with it."

Backing off, the wide-eyed girl shrugged out of her coat.

"You don't ever speak to me without permission," Ali growled, scowling.

Ashen faced, the girl draped the coat over the back of the low, white-cushioned sofa. Like every other piece of furniture in the room, its black wooden frame shouted of severity in the same way that Ali's appearance did.

Ali gave an inward smile of amusement. It was obvious from her trembling that the girl was intimidated by Ali's appearance, as she was indeed supposed to be. Visibly quaking, the poor young thing ran her eyes from Ali's black leather boots to her Basque. In response, Ali squared her narrow shoulders and set her expression sternly, turning black, hostile eyes upon the young trainee.

"Your name's Cindy, right?"

"Yes."

"I'm Mistress Blackheart, and that's what you'll call me."

Remembering her lessons, the girl gave a little curtsy. She focused her attention on the wicked looking whip which once again tap-tap-tapped against Ali's thigh, making the leather fronds jiggle menacingly.

As a soft, pink tint of embarrassment stained the girl's cheeks, Ali used the whip as a pointer, indicating the spot in the centre of the room where she was to stand. Impatient that the stupid girl still hadn't even started to take her clothes off, Ali regarded her coldly, making a silent appraisal of the shiny costume.

Made from purple PVC, it was an extremely sexy little number, consisting of a short skirt that barely covered her pubic mound, and a tiny bodice, linked to a matching collar by several short chains.

What a bloody waste! Ali thought, noting how the collar was purely decorative and served no real purpose. Her mind drifted back to the chateau, where the collars with which Chantel issued her slaves had many uses, one of which was as an effective means of constraint. But more importantly, in Ali's view, was the collar's usefulness in instilling a slave with the correct mental attitude; a collar that couldn't be removed by the wearer was a very potent reminder of a slave's inferiority, thereby reinforcing the supremacy of his betters.

"Quickly, girl", Ali snapped belligerently. "I told you to strip so get on with it, or you'll soon find out just how black my heart really is!"

The effect on Ali of the blushing girl's increasingly ham-fisted attempts to hurry was twofold. Firstly, it caused her impatience to turn to anger. Secondly, it set off the familiar, agitated quivers inside her that heralded her growing, gnawing arousal. Fingers of lust reached out and closed around her hardened heart.

Under Ali's forebodingly dark, imperious gaze, Cindy raised her slender, swanlike arms to undo the back fastening of the collar, her flush deepening with shame. And for Ali, that made the whole thing somehow even more exciting. She sucked in one cheek and with scorn and appreciation in equal parts, watched Cindy's obviously pained striptease.

In all honesty, the kid wasn't a bad looker, Ali allowed graciously as she watched Cindy's trembling fingers pluck clumsily at the bodice's fastening, at last removing the garment and throwing it aside. To Ali's delight, the small, perfectly round breasts were tipped with unexpectedly large, deep pink, puckered nipples.

When her clumsy fumbling had finally defeated the its zip, the skirt glided down around Cindy's legs to settle at her ankles. Slowly, she slid the matching panties down her legs and stepped from them.

"Who shaves your pussy?" Ali enquired phlegmatically, even though her heart was beating nineteen to the dozen.

"I do..." Cindy paused before adding, "Mistress" as if it were painful to even utter the name.

"By choice?" It would probably need doing every day to keep it smooth. Ali greedily feasted her eyes on the girl's small but beautifully flushed labia. Her exquisite slit was clearly defined, and there was already a tell-tale glistening of moisture, despite Cindy's apparent reluctance to co-operate.

"No, Mistress. My new Master ordered it."

Jeeeeez! To poke her fingers up inside Cindy's tight little love channel! It was with extreme reluctance that Ali tore her eyes away.

Ignoring the demands of her own sensuous, body, Ali settled herself in her favourite chair, the whip still firmly clasped in her hand. Leaning back into the oversized cushions, she took up her favourite pose with her arms resting on the chair's black wooden arms. Without hesitation or consideration for Cindy's fragile sensibilities, she spread her legs wide to fully reveal her own, black-thatched pussy. With a swift Crack! of the whip against the side of the chair, she barked her order.

"Kneel."

Obediently, Cindy settled herself on her knees between Ali's leather-clad legs and was completely at a loss as to why the mistress seemed even more waspish than before; she hadn't the faintest idea what she'd done to offend her.

Ali's lip curled into something like a smile. The girl's heart would be thumping by now in agitation, and she welcomed the light of terror that shone in Cindy's eyes as they met her own cold, black gaze. Doing her best to keep the laughter from her voice, Ali addressed the girl crisply.

"I thought you'd been taught at least a dash of respect - it seems I've been misinformed."

Ali raised the whip and brought it crashing down with an expertise that curled the fronds savagely around Cindy's waist to lash her unblemished back.

Yowling like a street cat as fire stung her soft, naked flesh, at once Cindy remembered how she'd been taught the correct position of submission. Obediently, she bowed her head and crossed her hands behind her back.

Putting as much derision into her tone as she was able, Ali said, "so, you're an inexperienced little tart that's only used to fucking men, right?"

Ali knew it was, but the thought of hearing Cindy's admission added to the thrill, in the same way that the recognition of her supremacy by the correct use of her title always did. Power was the thing, and the shame it generated in her slaves and lovers alike was a drug to which she was addicted.

"You've never been with a woman; never sucked her tits or stuck your fingers up her quim. Huh! You've no idea what you're missing."

She held her breath and waited, and was rewarded with the delightfully quivering voice of the frightened girl.

"Y... yes, I mean no, Mistress B...Blackheart." Caught by the light, Cindy's tears sparkled as they trickled from the corners of her innocent eyes.

Electric charges ricocheted throughout Ali's body. Hell! It was so good to have reduced her to tears. And this early in the proceedings! And as Cindy neared the edge of falling to pieces, Ali determined to extract as much pleasure as possible from the inexperienced young girl who knelt between her legs.

"Stop snivelling. It won't get you anywhere with me. I'm here to do a job, nothing more. This new master of yours, a guy you've yet to meet, is a man of considerable wealth and power. The thing is this - he's got a strong urge to see his recent acquisition," Ali tapped the handle of the whip on Cindy's bowed head, "namely you, make love to another woman. He also wants you flogged and fucked by other men. What he'll get when I've finished with you is a submissive slut who obeys orders and accepts punishment without complaint. Luckily for me, he hasn't got the guts to train you himself!"

Ali had no time for people with a hankering to see their slaves covered with criss-cross ridges, but hadn't the stomach to administer the blows themselves. She'd met people who, while demanding that their slave be beaten every day so as never to let the marks fade, couldn't bring themselves to perform the task themselves. It was almost inconceivable to Ali that anyone in such a position of power would deny themselves the pleasure of administering pain - for her it was the best aphrodisiac of all.

Therefore, she had no qualms about what she was doing, nor her client's motives; it didn't matter that she'd not met the individual concerned and was fully aware that she'd not been his first choice. Initially, he'd contacted his friend, the White Goddess to discuss the possibility of sending Cindy to be trained at the chateau. It was Chantel herself who'd recommended Ali, her own protégé, with the endorsement that she was a strict tutor, a harsh disciplinarian with a will of iron.

And so it had been decided. Cindy would be delivered to Ali once a week. While training the youngster for a reasonable fee, as an added incentive she was at liberty to use the girl in any way she saw fit. She'd opted to keep her for one or two nights, then ring to have the chauffeur take her away again.

It seemed the perfect arrangement, and one she intended to exploit to the full. Besides, she thought lecherously, it would be useful preparation for the seduction of Leigh.

Eager to wring every delicious drop of humiliation from the girl between her knees, Ali continued, colouring her language accordingly. "So, you've never fucking tasted the sweetness of a woman's fluids. Then it's time to start your lessons, you whore of a chickenheart.." Guessing correctly that Cindy blanched at the more emphatic turn of phrase gave Ali an extra kick. Hell! This was so much fun, it was almost more than she deserved... almost. "Lick me out, bitch! Suck the juices from my cunt."

Mortified, Cindy knelt with her mouth agape.

"Well? Haven't you got a tongue in that empty little head of yours? Use it, or I'll beat you so hard you won't be able to stand for a week, let alone sit down. Lick me!"

"Please, Mistress," Cindy's whimpering was an engaging blend of misery and pleading, "don't ask me to do it."

"I'm not bloody asking! " Holding the whip's stubby handle so tightly that her long nails dug into her palm, Ali raised the whip threateningly, "I'm ordering. Eat pussy - now!"

Knots of arousal tangled then unravelled in Ali's insides, triggering her sadistic nature. Her glossed, thin lips twitched and her black heart lurched as Cindy's hot tears of humiliation underwent a change from to a trickle to a downpour over her ever pinkening cheeks.

Long ago cleansed of all feelings of guilt, Ali's response to the youngster's shame was to wallow in the sheer joy of power that surged in hot torrents through her veins. Her clitoris pounded enthusiastically in anticipation of the delights to come. She must have done something pretty good in a past life to entitle her to such wholly erotic joys now... or something pretty bad. Either way, she hovered on the brink of ecstasy.

As Cindy obediently dipped her head toward Ali's black-fleeced sex, Ali set the narrow-thonged whip down across her lap. Using two fingers she opened her own engorged labia to reveal the red inner lips. Grabbing the back of Cindy's head she fiercely ground the girl's face against her moist slit.

Tentatively, Cindy flicked out her tongue and tasted Ali's musky, yet strangely fruity juices, her nose buried in Ali's thick pubes. She retched hopelessly at first, but a censuring dig in the ribs from Ali's spike heeled boot soon cured that. And when Ali removed her fingers, Cindy began licking the fleshy, elongated outer lips with long, slow strokes. With her knees wide apart and her own pussy beginning to moisten, Cindy shuffled closer, her knees sticking to the polished floorboards.

Snatching up the whip once more, Ali encouraged her with a sharp flick across her back. Cindy's response was immediate and she pushed the tip of her hot tongue into Ali's tight, lubricating channel.

Languishing in the erotic warmth that reverberated through her in tiny shock waves, Ali allowed herself a moment's delusion, imagining it was Leigh who tongued her rather than the stupid little blonde. She closed her eyes and luxuriated in sensations that the delightfully warm, wet tongue engendered, turning her insides to liquid fire.

Oh, if only it were Leigh that knelt submissively between her legs! To have Leigh submit to slavery, pleasuring her Mistress with her soft, pliant lips and snaking carnal tongue - that would be the greatest conquest of all! Of course, Leigh's first attempts would be equally as clumsy as Cindy's; her inexperience would soon earn her the punishment Ali had craved to deliver for so many years, and it would be all the more sweet for it.

A bolt of electricity shot from Ali's nipples to her wonderfully teased sex. Her breaths came out raggedly as she imagined the rapture of seeing Leigh in cruel bondage in the playroom, bondage that was becoming all the more certain by the moment. The thought made her shudder and, nearing her peak, she fought to hold it back, knowing that when it finally came it would have been worth the postponement.

As Cindy's efforts increased, so Ali's thoughts of domination over Leigh soared to new heights. Her long held fantasy took on a more structured shape as she laid the foundations of Leigh's complete subjugation. Ali's roots went back a long way in this town, and were inexorably entwined with Leigh's - so it was only right that she should dominate her - make her suffer. After all, that's why she'd come home.

"Push your tongue deeper, lick me out as if your life depended upon it."

Breathlessly, Ali issued her commands, the veins in her neck standing out tautly as her head went back. Already she could feel the tension mounting, mounting, and mounting; a glorious tension that needed relief - now!

"Put some effort into it or I'll flay the skin from your back!"

Still pressing Cindy's face firmly between her legs to prevent the girl from escaping, Ali scrunched Cindy's hair tightly in her fingers. She'd die if the stupid bimbo didn't make her come soon.

Cindy curled her tongue and thrust it deeper, making a little noise of surprise as Ali's muscles clenched tightly around it. Wiggling her tongue daintily, she thrust it in and out, trying to build up a rhythm that would earn Mistress Blackheart's respect.

Under Cindy's inept yet wholly erotic ministrations, Ali's passion rocketed sky high and her spirits danced, while the thoughts that crammed her brain had her bucking and writhing. Panting as Cindy continued to tongue her, she reached out for the youngster's breast, squeezing the small but exquisite orb so roughly that Cindy groaned her protests against the wet warmth of Ali's vagina.

"Stop whining, you pathetic little whore, or I'll give you something to whine about!"

Teetering on the brink of orgasm, Ali was going mad with need. Releasing her hold on the back of Cindy's head, she seized Cindy's nipples, now surprisingly long and hard, between finger and thumb. But it wasn't only Cindy who screamed.

"No more! Bring me to climax, Slut! Do it, or I'll twist your nipples off!"

As if to carry out her threat, Ali twisted them so sadistically that the girl jerked backward, snatching her mouth from Ali's pussy. The sight of Cindy's nose, mouth and chin glistening with her juices set Ali's heart pounding with the primitive beat of a lioness. Her muscles clutched at nothing as the unbearable need for relief drove her frantic. God! She really was going to die! Her hand darted out and, after delivering a stinging blow across Cindy's cheek, she grabbed the back of her neck and thrust Cindy's head back between her legs. Her strong fingers once again closed over Cindy's tortured nipples. Twisting them as if trying to wring nectar from them, Ali felt such an explosion of joy that she actually whooped with delight, exulting at the muffled yelp of pain against her mound.

Then, without being told to, Cindy extracted her tongue and sought out the hard bud at the apex of Ali's labia. She flicked at the hard morsel of flesh, taking it between her teeth and giving little nips that had Ali groaning deliriously.

The whip clattered to the floor. Tremors wracked Ali's body as at last she underwent the fierce cramps and spasms of orgasm. Her legs shot out rigid as, with her eyes tightly closed, her head thrown back and her mouth wide, she gave a howl that shook her whole body. Not since leaving the chateau had she had such a powerful climax.

Cindy detached her mouth gently. With her face covered in Ali's musky secretions, she looked on and marvelled at the transformation. And if Ali could have read her mind, she'd have known that Cindy had noted that Mistress Blackheart had a weakness after all.

***

Leigh rubbed the sex-induced sleep from her eyes. In the glare from the hall light she unlocked the front door, keeping the security chain in place. She peered out through the narrow opening into the darkness.

"Owen! What the hell are you doing here? It's late."

His ravaging eyes took in the way she flaunted her curves through her nightdress, so transparent it was virtually invisible. She was up for it all right! He could tell by the way her nipples, red and hard, poked against the fabric; she was the hottest little number it had been his pleasure to fuck for a long time. And, since the scheming bitch thought she had some kind of hold over him, he was determined to get his money's worth.

"Let me in."

"I can't." Her heart pounded in her ribcage, not just from fear but also the excitement of Errol coming down and discovering them. She looked at him coquettishly, wet her lips, then whispered "I'm not alone."

"I'm not here to discuss your sleeping arrangements, Sweetheart." He didn't shout. In some ways that was worse. "Let me in, now."

His softly spoken words carried a hint of menace that should have put her on her guard. Instead, she unhooked the chain. He shoved past her, knocking the door backward so that she was squashed behind it against the wall. Like a bully in the school playground, he barged his way into her hallway.

"I want you to go." She was irritated now as she watched him opening doors and peering inside. "I'll see you in the morning, Owen."

"You'll see me now! "

With a look of resignation, Leigh closed the door.

Errol's sleep-laden voice came from the top of the stairs. "Leigh? What's going on?" when she didn't answer, he tried again, this time more forcefully. "Leigh! Are you all aright? Who is it?"

Owen wasn't about to have his pleasure curtailed by some layabout she hung around with. In a flash, he grabbed her wrist and dragged it up between her shoulder blades.

"Answer him, Bitch!" he hissed venomously.

Grimacing with pain, she thought it better to do what he said before he really hurt her.

"Everything's ok. I'll..." It was all going wrong! "I'll be up in a minute."

"Are you sure everything's ok, Leigh?"

"Not very brave, is he, this lover of yours?" Owen sneered, pulling her wrist higher and making her give a little cry. "You'd think he'd have the balls to come down and check."

"Leigh?"

"Make up an excuse; say you're just getting a drink of water."

Wincing with pain, she trilled "Go back to bed. It was just my neighbour, checking to see if I'd seen his cat."

"At half past two?"

"He's a light sleeper. It's ok, he's gone now. I'm just going to the kitchen for a drink of water."

"Don't be long, Baby. The bed's getting cold."

She heard Errol's footsteps padding back across the landing above her as he returned to the bedroom. Visibly trembling now, she was scared and angry. But the clutching of her pussy hinted at a far more enjoyable state of affairs - surely she wasn't aroused?

Still holding her arm tightly between her shoulders, Owen manhandled her into the living room. Hissing threats under his breath, he fumbled for the lights switch. He flipped it on, kicked the door closed, then threw her face down on the couch. She turned her head and gave a quick glance over her shoulder to see him standing over her, unzipping his fly.

"I've been thinking about you," the last remnants of malice drained from his voice as he continued in a softer tone that was almost good humoured, "all day. I can't get enough of you, you horny little minx."

This was more like the other Owen, the one she liked to lead on. Turning onto her back, she sprawled against the sofa. She couldn't get rid of him, so she might as well enjoy it. With Errol upstairs, things could get very interesting, and the thought of having two men at the same time filled her head with amazing possibilities... one in her sex and one in her mouth... her innards tingled in anticipation. She was probably making another mistake, but what the hell! The joy of sending a man wild with desire was just too good to resist.

"Ok, big boy," she invited in the teasing way she knew he liked, "come and get it." She crossed her arms in front as, arching her back, she pulled the nightdress off over her head. "It's playtime."

In a moment he was on her, clutching her breasts, his cock fumbling like that of an overeager adolescent at the entrance of her tight, moistening channel. Leigh closed her elegantly tapering fingers around his quiveringly stiff shaft and guided it towards its prize. As the silky-skinned crown nudged her labia apart, she drew in an exaggerated, tremulous breath.

"Oooooh, Owen," she giggled in the young, tinkling voice she knew drove him wild. "You're so big!" Thrusting her hips upward to assist him, she lied shamelessly as his cock pushed past her inner lips into the warm depths. "I've never been fucked by anyone as big as you."

The little bitch was driving him insane. His hands gripped her shoulders as he pounded into her. He groaned incoherent words of lust, relishing the squirming of her tender, young body beneath his weight. He loved the way she entwined his hair with her fingers, opening her soft mouth to emit breathless sighs.

Leigh smiled inwardly. There was nothing like a bit of teasing to get the juices flowing, but the notion that he took her seriously had her stifling her giggles. Determined to put on a good show, she writhed enthusiastically, bucking her hips as his hard pounding announced his urgent need. It felt so good to have a man want her so badly.

"Ooooo!"

Now she was really getting turned on! Tingles and quivers assailed her body, sending familiar sensations shivering from her sensitized breasts to her vulva.

"Aaaaah!"

She hardly noticed the shift from enjoyment to discomfort. It was a gradual process that was dulled by the haze in her mind. His heavy, rasping breath warmed her face as his head moved closer to hers. It was strange how his weight seemed to increase with his urge, she thought distractedly as he opened his lips. She parted hers in reply.

Then his hard mouth crushed down on hers, depriving her of precious air. His balls slapped against her as he used his penis like a weapon, plunging deep, so deep that it hurt her insides. She was uncomfortable. She couldn't breathe, and he jabbed into her so fiercely that she'd have cried out were she able to breathe.

It dawned on her then that there was a change; that her arousal had been supplanted by panic rising in her stomach, along with foul tasting bile.

Still she couldn't breathe. If he didn't get off her, the bile in her throat would explode into her mouth. Oh the shame! She wouldn't be able to stop it! He had to get off her!

As his body grew even heavier, she slid her hands down between their two bodies. Struggling for air, she strove to push him off. When that didn't work, she extracted her hands again and began to pound his back with her fists for all she was worth.

At last he pulled away from her and she gulped in lungfuls of air.

"What are you struggling for, Sweetheart? You know it's what you want."

"Get off me! You're hurting me."

"I haven't even started yet."

"Owen, get off me. I feel sick."

Her pelvic bone felt bruised, and he was gripping her shoulders so tightly it felt as if he were pushing her though the springs of the sofa onto the floor below. What on earth had made her trust him in the first place? Threats, pain - she should have known better; the man was nothing but a bully.

It was almost physical as something inside her snapped, like the breaking of a tendon or crack of the ribs.

"I said 'get off me!'"

She dredged up every last ounce of energy and willpower within her. First, she tensed her muscles then suddenly, in one swift movement that caught him off guard she brought up her knee and caught him in the balls. His yell was like a wounded animal. His eyes filled with water as he pulled out of her, clutching at his crotch.

"You fucking bitch!" He was on his feet with the speed of a younger man. With his lip curling menacingly, he looked down at her with a distaste that curdled her blood. "I'll see you pay for this, whore."

"Get out of my house, or I'll shame you in front of everyone. And don't think I won't! I'll tell the other doctors first thing in the morning."

"Not Errol Proudfoot, you won't - he's at a conference in Blackpool."

Owen was definitely shaken; Leigh couldn't help but notice the uncertainty in his voice as he continued his ranting. "Terence Rankin wouldn't believe you anyway, his wife Claire is a great friend of my wife's, so you see, no one would believe you. You're treading on dangerous ground, young lady. One word from you in the wrong place, and you'll be out on your ear."

Leigh's fists were white-knuckled with anger as she clenched them at her sides. She sucked on her bottom lip, took a deep breath and, mentally drawing herself up to her full height, let him have it right between the eyes.

"Your threats aren't worth the breath it takes to make them. Mine, on the other hand, are far more serious. I could destroy you, your career, your marriage - so perhaps it's you that should watch your step, Dr. Brand."

"You wouldn't dare!"

It was at that moment that Errol chose to leap from the bed and Owen swerved his eyes toward the ceiling as they heard his footsteps pad across the floor

There was as much venom in Leigh's voice now as there'd been come-on before. She recalled the time years ago when Ali had made her carry out her threat, spoken in the heat of the moment, to falsely accuse a fellow student of cheating during exams. Though nothing was ever proved against him, the boy's reputation had been ruined. She'd been wrong back then, of course, but this time round she had right on her side.

"If that's what you think, Owen, you don't know me very well. I don't know what the hell you came round here for- I told you I didn't want a relationship. Now get out, before I do something I'll really regret!"

Still clutching at his balls, Owen made for the door. Wrenching it open, he staggered down the hallway and headed for the front door without a backward glance.

He left it wide open, filling the hall with damp night air, and had melted into the night before Leigh had even raised herself off the sofa.

After locking up again and replacing the security chain, Leigh leant against the door to regain her breath. She didn't know what she was going to do about Owen, but it was too late to think about it now; she had work in the morning.

Without meaning them to, thoughts of Ali fluttered unannounced into her head. She smiled a capricious smile, doubting that even Ali, despite her brash, big talk, had had such an eventful night.

With the thought of poor Ali sleeping cold and alone uppermost in her mind, she headed back up the stairs. Errol was on his way down.

"Everything all right, Baby?"

"Yes thanks. I couldn't sleep, so I turned on the TV. It was some sixties horror film. You know the sort of thing, all busty blondes screaming their guts up and guys with dripping fangs and billowing cloaks. I gave up with it." She trudged past him, not waiting as he fell into step behind her. "What time do you leave for Blackpool in the morning?"

CHAPTER FIVE

With her small hands on her hips and a cigar between her fingers, Ali stood over the still kneeling figure.

"Look at me," her tone was low, silky-smooth and unfeeling, "I'm going to beat you." She was fully aware that her words, when spoken in such a fashion, sent chills straight to the heart. Once again she relished the surge of power that swept over her, and the look of naked terror in Cindy's eyes. "Has anyone ever beaten you before?"

"N... no, Mistress."

"Blackheart!" Ali grabbed the girl by the arm and hauled her roughly to her feet. "Say it girl, and tremble."

"Mistress Blackheart."

"That's better. Go and stand behind the chair." She stubbed out her cigar against the white wall - Jurgen could clean it up in the morning - while she waited for the terrified girl to comply. "Good. Lean forward over the back and rest your hands on the seat cushion."

Again, Cindy did as she was bidden, pressing her smooth, naked belly against the chair back. Ali came up behind her then, with a ferocity that made Cindy stumble, she kicked her legs apart. Using the same kind of cord she'd used to bind Jurgen, she tied Cindy's ankles to the chair legs.

Scraping her fingers through her hair, Ali walked round to the front and used another length of the same cord to bind Cindy's wrists together. With a steely calm meant to intimidate, she gave the cord a sharp yank downward, at the same time pulling the youngster forward over the chair back, and her head down towards the seat. She splayed her fingers on the back of Cindy's head and ground her face down against the cushion. When she was satisfied with Cindy's position, she pulled on the cord once more, thus tugging Cindy's wrists down towards the floor. Hunkering down, Ali threaded the cord underneath the chair, again tugging at Cindy's wrists.

"You did well in your first lesson." Dropping the end of the cord with a "don't move!" Ali straightened up and walked back round behind Cindy. "But as I never dish out carrots to slaves - only the stick - your only reward for pleasing me will be that I might not thrash you quite so hard." She gave a chilling laugh, "but I'll make up for it on your next visit."

Bending from the waist, she snatched up the cord again and threaded it up between the back of the chair and Cindy's naked body, giving it a sharp jerk, making it chafe against Cindy's belly. Finally, she secured the cord to the back of the chair.

"Please-"

"Shut up!"

"Don't beat me, Mistress Blackheart, p... please."

"Shut it!"

Out of Cindy's line of vision, Ali went through to her bedroom and collected two Indian silk scarves from a drawer. Selecting a riding crop from a wall rack in her bedroom, where all kinds of whips, paddles and other paraphernalia were neatly rearranged daily by Jurgen, Ali returned to the frightened girl in the sitting room. Bunching up one of the scarves, she stuffed it in Cindy's mouth.

"As much as I'd love to hear you scream, it's past three in the morning and I don't want the neighbours complaining. In time, I'll have this whole place soundproofed, but for now we'll have to make do and mend."

Ali tied the other scarf across her mouth to keep it in place, then took up a position behind her. She cast her critical eyes over the swell of the small buttocks. Temptingly presented, there wasn't a great deal of flesh on them but they formed a rather nice heart shape, with a deep, inviting valley between.

Ali's breasts tightened. She always got turned on at the prospect of a good beating, and right now she was so turned on that it burnt her insides.

"Ok, where shall we begin?" Using the palm of her hand, Ali struck the girl's bottom and raised both an instant patch of very satisfying red, and a muffled cry into the gag, "here or..." she slapped Cindy's taut thigh, "here?"

Smiling at the stifled sobs that followed, Ali ran her eager fingers gently over the reddened flesh of Cindy's buttocks as if soothing away the pain. A frisson of heat set her pussy juicing at the mere prospect of inflicting even more pain on that sweet, tender flesh as she repeated the process with Cindy's thigh.

Standing with her legs apart, Ali tensed them for stability. Then, with lightning speed and a power to match, she brought the crop down, causing a line of fire to blaze across one cheek of Cindy's bottom. The small amount of flesh quivered pleasingly.

Ali's free hand sought out her own nipple. Rolling and squeezing the brown morsel of hardened flesh, she raised the crop and mentally measured the distance of her swing. She pinched her nipple harder, bit into her lip and then, with a force that drove chair and captive across the floor she struck again, this time across the other cheek.

Warming to her theme, as hard as she was able Ali squeezed and pinched her brown nipple excitedly and, before the young girl at her mercy could get her breath back, Ali had laid another vivid stripe over the first, followed in close succession by another across the other buttock.

And so it went on, strike after terrible strike that brought frenzied, stifled screams into the gag, and angry red weals to the soft, delicate skin. Hot rivers of tears cascaded down Cindy's face, hanging like diamonds from her chin before falling to dampen the chair cushion.

"Cry all you want," Ali told her as she found her rhythm, all the while squeezing her own nipple so much that it hurt, "but if it's sympathy you're after, you're in the wrong place."

***

It was morning before Ali returned to the playroom to check on Jurgen.

Standing in front of him with her small hands clasping a much-needed mug of coffee, she lifted it upward so that the aroma wafted towards his nose. "Tell me, how do you like the company?"

Still tethered to the wall bars, Jurgen flicked his eyes across the playroom to where the unfortunate Cindy was compelled to stand on tiptoe. Stark naked, gagged, and positioned facing him so that he had a perfect view of her small breasts and shaved pussy, her arms were stretched tautly above her head.

Shiny, metal handcuffs around her wrists were fastened to a black, metal beam that could be lowered from the ceiling by means of a pulley system. Extending from one side of the room to the other, it had been cleverly designed to be fixed in place by bolts at each end, which slotted into corresponding fixtures on the walls. Great care had gone into the design and construction of the room so that all such manoeuvres could easily be managed by Ali alone. And since she was only of average height, to make life easier there were step ladders tucked away in the corner.

Jurgen's considerable cock jerked involuntarily. As a horny male with red hot blood rampaging through his veins, it had been bad enough, as Ali had known it would be, to hear the activities from the adjoining room last night and not be able to watch, let alone participate. But now, the proximity of the delightful Cindy made things a hundred times worse.

"Please, Mistress," he pleaded, "don't beat her again."

Ali turned to admire her work. Weals of fiery red patterned the front of Cindy's thighs in a close-knit weave, as indeed they criss-crossed the back of them. Her small, heart-shaped bottom also had a network of angry weals to improve its appearance.

Ali smiled briefly, then turned back to Jurgen with her black eyes flashing.

"Don't be a sentimental fool! You know she deserved it. The girl was clumsy and useless. How am I ever going to get obedience from her without dishing out the discipline? You've seen girls beaten before at the chateau; what's so special about this one?"

"She's young, Mistress."

"Of course she's bloody young! She's nineteen, what difference does that make? You've seen them when they've been whipped until they couldn't stand, and still you've bayed for more." She narrowed her eyes, and there was an unflattering twist to her lips as she continued, "I know, Jurgen... I know your secret!"

Jurgen's head jerked up in response. The blood drained from his face as the reality he'd tried so hard to forget rose like a spectre to stare him in the face. The shame of what he'd once been, coupled with the humiliation of what he'd since become, was almost too much to bear. And the cold-hearted bitch knew it. He could see in her face how much she enjoyed his degradation.

"You dare to beg for mercy on her behalf! Hypocrite! You were one of the cruellest bastards alive until Chantel found and tamed you." She raised her black brows mockingly and twisted her thin upper lip. "The famous Jurgen, adored by thousands in your homeland for your feats of strength, were as sadistic as they come. A whip-wielding master who enslaved young girls, not much older than this one, and kept them in chains. I've heard about 'the wheel'." White-hot arousal tugged at the very root of her as her mind displayed the image, "a cruel, circular device to which you'd chain your young victims, spread-eagled like spokes in a wheel, before whipping them." Oh, if only she had the means to do the same! "Then you'd have the thing slotted between the shafts of a cart and wheeled around your grand estate for the other girls to see- until you lost your nerve. Now look at you. You're nothing! You're a wimp, half a man that can't stand up to a woman half his size. The lash tamed you..." she jabbed her thumb over her shoulder, "and it'll tame her!"

Jurgen hung his head as the heat of shame swept over him. It was true, all of it. After all this time, images of his girls still filled his head during the quiet times. If those girls could see him now, no longer a sadistic master but a humiliated slave like themselves, beaten for another's pleasure...

He hated to be this way; to long for Ali's words of reproach; to crave the strike of her cane on his flesh; to need her cruelty as much as he needed to breathe; to belong body and soul to Mistress Blackheart.

She took another sip of coffee.

"Poor Jurgen. You've been stuck there all night. I bet you're so bloody thirsty you think your throat's been cut!" She gave him that sneering smile. "Ask me nicely, and I might give you a sip."

Jurgen's fingers clenched into tight balls as the cord held his wrists fast, and he imagined it was her pretty neck that his fingers closed around. The bitch knew he was thirsty! His full lips were dry and his throat arid.

"Please, Mistress Blackheart, allow me a sip of your coffee."

Her harsh "No!" erupted on a cracked laugh.

While he looked on enviously, she finished what was left of it, holding the mug in one hand while she toyed with his cock with the other. She delighted in the way it stiffened to its full potential under her ministrations. Clasping it firmly, she scraped her long fingernails tantalizingly from its base to its crown. Slowly, she circled the weeping eye in its centre before running her fingers back down to its base. Clutching his balls, she gave them a spiteful squeeze that made him yelp like a dog in distress.

"Still thirsty, Jurgen?"

"Yes, Mistress."

With one quick flick of her wrist, she emptied the coffee grounds down the front of his magnificent chest. For a moment their eyes locked in battle - hers coal black and haughty, his clear blue and resentful. Then, slowly forced to submit, Jurgen lowered his gaze to the floor.

Tossing the empty mug over her shoulder, it smashed into several pieces as it landed on the gleaming white floorboards.

"Clean it up later," she instructed

Gripping hold of his shoulder, which still smarted from the cigar burn, Ali raised her leg and rested her booted foot on the wall bar, beside his chunky thigh. Then, she released his shoulder and made a grab with both hands for the bars on either side of his head, hoisting up her other leg. With a foot on either side of him, she began to climb upward.

Now, with her feet either side of his head, she used the spiked heels of her boots to dig into his shoulder blades, forcing him to ease forward to try and evade the discomfort. When she was satisfied with the result, she hooked her legs over his shoulders. Easing them down his back, she sat with her musky, naked crotch pressed firmly against his neck so that her dark thatch, glistening with beads of moisture, tickled the underside of his chin.

She eased herself back a notch. With the sharp command, "lick my cunt!" she gripped the bars tightly and leaned backwards, stretching her arms tautly, before lifting herself slightly off his shoulders. She raised her hips and presented her open, moistening vagina to his mouth, crossing her legs behind his back. Her hands let go of the bars and she hung like a rag doll, supported by his shoulders.

Hungrily he fell upon her, flicking his tongue over her desire-hardened clitoris. Swirls of thrilling agitation made her body tremble, engendering a wild, fiery excitement that made her cry out.

His cock twitched as his own excitement increased. She was a bitch, a wicked witch of a bitch - and an angel - black hearted but an angel nonetheless. He thrust his tongue past her inner lips, deep into her tight depths and tasted her sweetness, like fruits in a musky coating. God how he hated her- and worshipped her- and revelled in the licentiousness of it all.

Her inner muscles clamped tightly around his thick, hot tongue, trying to milk it as she'd milk his cock. A frisson of white hot arousal built up to feverish need. She tensed. She screamed. She almost fell.

As her second devastating orgasm within hours shook her to the core, Jurgen's hot sperm fountained across the room to form another puddle.

For a few moments they remained like that, mistress and slave locked together in a moment of understanding. Each knew their place and the invisible line that separated them remained intact.

Once she'd fully recovered and regained an upright position, still sitting on his shoulder, she worked to release his bonds.

"Clean this mess up, Jurgen, then get a couple of hours sleep. I want her -" she jerked her head toward Cindy, "fed and watered. Afterwards, clean her up and ring to have her collected. I don't want to see her again until next week." She looked over her shoulder and addressed Cindy coldly. "Next time, I'll teach you what real punishment is."

CHAPTER SIX

"Good morning, Leigh." Dr. Rankin flashed her a smile.

Leigh flashed a leg in return as she swivelled round in her chair to face him across the cramped office. Sitting with her back to the reception desk behind the glass partition, she treated him to her sexiest smile, like a kitten at play.

"Good morning, Terence."

Her light, musical voice belied the anxiety behind her smile, just as the mischief that danced in her pale, grey-green eyes belied the dread in the pit of her stomach. The thought of seeing Owen this morning had given her a bad taste in the mouth. She'd even considered calling in sick, but with the other receptionist still off, there'd have been no one to mind shop. Besides, if she had taken a sickie, it would have meant that Owen had won. She'd just have to grit her teeth and get on with it.

Perhaps things might not be so bad, she thought as Terence Rankin sifted through a pile of patients' notes; maybe there was fun to be had here this morning after all. Her lips curved into a smile of anticipation, and she ran the tip of her tongue over her front teeth. Of course, what she'd really like to run her tongue over was the shiny helmet of his cock.

Terence replaced the notes on the shelf and turned round to face her again. She sat back and opened her legs just a touch. Though barely enough to make her short skirt ride up, it was enough to bring a sparkle to his eyes and a thrill quivering through her.

"How are you this morning, Terence?" Her voice, once again like that of a younger girl as she flicked the mischief switch, was light and tinkling.

"Better for seeing you," he laughed.

In his fifties, friendly and with a pair of gold rimmed specs perched on his hawk nose, he was probably the most considerate, kindest of the three doctors. He was married, with two grown-up children. Leigh had been at school with one of his sons, who'd suffered terribly at Ali's hands but had always seemed to come back for more. And Leigh had had a brief fling with his other son last year, before sending him scampering back to his newly-wed wife.

Terence watched as Leigh wet her lips with the tip of her tongue. As if trying to ease a pain in her chest, using her open palm she stroked her right hand across the front of her flimsy blouse. Opening and closing her fingers, she rubbed back and forth, making sure she 'accidentally' caught the engorged nipple of her left breast with her little finger. The performance wasn't lost on Terence, whose Adams apple looked as if it had stuck in his throat when he tried to swallow.

Using her other hand, Leigh stroked her inner thigh through the fabric of her skirt. She batted her eyelids a couple of times for good measure, then treated Terence to her wide-eyed look of innocence. She flicked her eyes downward, focussing on his crotch. To her joy he was clearly getting the message. How on earth was he going to hide that bulge from his patients? she thought wickedly.

The idea of a shocked patient excited her even more, and the devil in her prompted her to prolong his agony. She gave a wistful sigh, then opened her lips and made a show of running the tip of her tongue back and forth over her top lip. Her breasts tightened beneath her blouse, and that made her nipples stiffen even more.

Delighting in the sweet sensations of arousal that fluttered through her, it gave her a real buzz to see Terence fidget with the collar of his shirt as he tried to keep from giving in to his very apparent needs. He wanted her, just as he'd done since she'd first come to work at the practice. And she wanted him, but only as long as he was off-limits.

Terence cleared his throat. "It's nearly nine o'clock. You'd better open the gates to the hordes. Don't forget that Dr. Proudfoot's gone to a conference in Blackpool."

"Ok, Doctor."

How could she, since she was the one who'd waved him off at 6.30 that morning?

"By the way," Terence's hand moved surreptitiously to the front of his trousers as he endeavoured to rearrange himself more comfortably, "Owen rang me to say he's going to be a bit late this morning." Lowering his voice to a conspiratorial whisper, he winked as he added "a bit of domestic trouble."

"Oh, right," she said, noncommittally, thanking God for small mercies.

She pushed back her chair and eased herself to her feet, watching as Terence made for the safety of his consulting room at the far end of the corridor. Giggling, she called after him.

"The other receptionist is still off sick - there's only you and me here. Who knows what mischief we could get up to?"

"Quite. Open the doors, Leigh."

Still giggling, she walked across to the front entrance and stooped down to undo the bolt at the bottom of the door. Straightening up, she silently lamented the fact that Owen would be in at all, and ruin any chance she had of slipping into Terence's consulting room after surgery. From the look of his bulge, it was her guess that he had a pretty good piece of equipment tucked away.

Reaching upward, she drew down the second bolt. She swung the door open and stood aside to let the first of the patients inside.

"Ali!"

***

Nina Brand looked down at her husband with an accusatory gaze. She didn't hate him, nor did she love him. She wasn't sure when it had happened, but love had moved out at some point during their marriage and had been replaced by a nondescript feeling that had left her dead inside. So she was surprised at the sudden depth of feeling his latest infidelity had inflicted upon her. It shouldn't matter, not now that she had... she smiled inwardly... interests of her own. But it did matter, and she wanted him to pay.

She didn't know how she knew there was someone new on the scene, she just did. It was a kind of sixth sense, she guessed, that she'd honed to perfection. It was this sense that had first set off the alarm the other day, when she'd met Owen after morning surgery.

She rarely met with her husband socially. Other than the necessary, periodical rounds of bank managers, solicitors and other officials, they were seldom seen together in public, except for some evening engagement for which Owen needed the extra appendage of a dutiful wife.

"Coffee, Owen?"

Despite the sudden re-emergence of feeling, she employed another of the polished performances she'd perfected to shield herself, by keeping her voice flat and emotionless. Standing by the side of his chair, she gripped the coffee pot so tightly that her fingers turned white. Of course, if she were to accidentally-on-purpose spill it...

Owen folded his morning paper and laid it down on the breakfast table. Without a word or even the briefest of glances to acknowledge his wife's presence on the planet, he slid his empty coffee cup from its set position to the corner of the table where she stood.

If there was one thing Nina hated, it was being ignored. Her bottom lip quivered as she struggled to keep the floodgates closed on the unshed tears of years. How was it, she wondered, that after all this time that he still had the power to hurt her? Why did she even care? She promised herself that she'd somehow find a way to make him pay for the years of emptiness.

Once again she considered the consequences of pouring the hot liquid over him, toyed with the idea of humiliating him by sending him to work in a dirty shirt. Except that he had a drawer full of clean ones. What she'd really like to do was go upstairs and toss them all out of the window and into the street below. She'd like the good people of this town to know what a louse the good doctor really was!

Coming out of her brief reverie, she filled his cup before walking back across the kitchen. Plonking the coffee pot down on the worktop, she stood with her back towards him.

"What did you tell Terence that for?" she busied herself with the usual, unnecessary tidying up before the cleaning lady arrived. "What on earth will he think?"

Owen still didn't look at her as he buttered his toast. But then, he hardly ever looked at her. His wife had ceased to amuse him years ago. While he'd be the first to acknowledge that she had a better than average figure, some would say she could have made a fortune by posing for the camera, he'd always found her lovemaking rather mechanical.

"I don't give a shit what Terence thinks! I told him the truth, that I'm running late and that my wife and I are having problems. Heaven knows there's never been anything else but problems in our marriage. For the first time he looked at her, "and I don't like your sneaking down the stairs to listen to my private calls."

Gripped by an overflowing of pent-up emotions, Nina swung round with a wooden spatula in her hand. She pointed it at him as she spoke, anger glinted in her eyes like hot coals.

"I remind you, Owen, that Daddy bought this house. I don't have to sneak anywhere. Unlike you, creeping in at all hours of the morning. Who is she this time, another patient? One of those sweet young things that comes to you for contraceptive advice? You'll be struck off one of these days!"

"I wouldn't have to go elsewhere if you were a real wife! When was the last time you opened your legs for me?" He turned his attention back to the breakfast table and reached for the marmalade.

Nina ignored the remark. "As for listening to your calls, how could I help but overhear when the phone's on the hall table at the bottom of the stairs? You were already speaking to Terence as I came down."

"You were eavesdropping! Besides, if you hadn't been so late getting up," he dug his knife around the bottom of the marmalade jar, "you would've already been in the bloody kitchen."

He spread the remains of the marmalade over his toast, took a bite, then continued.

"What kind of wife are you? You've got cleaning ladies, gardeners, even someone to collect and return the dry cleaning! What bloody use are you? What the fuck do you do all day? Sit on your lazy backside gossiping with your hoity-toity friends from the Ladies Of Overseas Charity League? Huh! The most you've ever raised for charity is your skirt for the chairman at last year's Doctors Benevolent Fund dinner." He glanced at the kitchen clock. "You're a waste of space as a wife.

You know I'm due at the surgery- the fucking least you could do of a morning is prepare a decent breakfast."

Nina stalked back across the kitchen towards him, spatula in hand. Raising it as she drew alongside him, for a moment it hovered in mid air above his head. She took a deep breath and lowered her arm. One of these days she'd teach him a lesson. Walking round the table she threw the spatula aside, pulled out the chair opposite him and sat down.

"If you don't like the way I run things around here, you can move out. But you won't do that, will you, not while my money's funding your little jaunts! Incidentally, I know about the earrings."

"What earrings?" His face was a picture of innocence as he took another bite.

Nina laughed bitterly. She watched as he put the toast on his plate to sip from his coffee cup.

"The ones you bought at that high class London jeweller's last month. It was careless of you to leave the receipt in the writing bureau. Who were they for," she tried to gauge his reaction as he replaced the cup and reached for his toast, "that little trollop you've had stashed away on Tewkesbury Street for the past three years?"

His hand froze midway between his plate and his mouth. How long had she known?

"God only knows what they see in you, Owen. You look like a bloody goldfish!" She inhaled deeply to steady herself before dropping the bombshell. "I want a divorce."

His reaction wasn't the one she'd anticipated. He merely laughed, almost choking on his toast in the process.

"Now I know you're joking! Think of the scandal. You see, I've got something on you, too." He waited the briefest moment before continuing. "What would Claire Rankin and your other friends at the Choral Society say, or your pals from the Pony Club, if they were to find out about your little... fling... with the Reverend Sophie Boyd? Or that young chap... what's his name? Ah yes, Kevin, the eighteen year old across the street. No, I think our marriage is safe for the time being."

"We don't stone unfaithful wives in this town!" Inwardly, she gave a sigh of relief, As long as he didn't find out about her other little predilections she could maybe bluff it out. Either that or she'd have to forfeit the house and leave him. "If it's good enough for you..."

"Don't give me that, Nina! At least I don't fuck with my own kind. You like your bread buttered both sides. Women like you make me sick. What are you, some church-trawling dyke, or a cradle-snatching pervert?"

He snatched up the marmalade jar. Drawing back his arm, before she had time to react he flung it at her, catching her squarely on the jaw.

"Bastard!" She cupped her face in her hand, as if that could somehow take the pain away, and closed her eyes.

Beside her in an instant, Owen kicked at her chair.

"Get up! Spread your legs and see what it's like to be fucked by a man!"

She opened her eyes, and was struck by the glittering rage in his. She hadn't seen him this angry for years. Easing back her chair, Nina stood up. If only there were some way to teach him a lesson.

Owen dragged the chair away with such force that it fell and clattered to the floor.

"Lean forward, with your hands on the table."

When she didn't comply, he put a hand in the small of her back and shoved her forward, so that her full breasts were flattened against the table. Before she had time to straighten up, he yanked down the zip of his trousers. He leant forward, and with one hand between her shoulder blades, he held her down and used his other hand to hike her pleated skirt up around her waist. He dragged her panties down to her knees.

With his mouth open, he inhaled deeply. It was so long since he'd seen any part of her naked that he was immediately struck by the beauty of her fleshy buttocks, separated into two perfect globes by a deep channel.

He extracted his throbbing, rigid penis from his spotted boxer shorts. With both hands, he made a grab at her backside. Quivering flesh spilled over his hands. Lust heated his balls and surged upward as he thrust his hips forward. His cock disappeared between the fleshy cheeks and nudged against the tight, puckered skin, demanding entry.

"No, Owen, please..."

"Don't tell me it's still a virgin hole!"

"You do this to me, and I'll..."

"Don't threaten me! You're my wife and from now on, you're going to give me exactly what I want."

He moved his hands to her hips and gripped her tightly. Without thought of lubrication, in one swift movement he lunged forward. She screamed in agony as the tip of his cock broached the barrier. Fire lit up her entire back passage as his shaft buried itself up to the hilt in her backside.

"You bastard!" Nina clenched her teeth and screwed up her eyes in an effort to endure the pain. "You'll pay for this!"

As suddenly as he'd thrust his cock in, he extracted it. Again she screamed, the agony as great on the way out as it had been on the way in.

Still gripping her with one hand, he delved between her thighs with the other and parted her labia.

"You're wet! You want it as much as I do."

"Not with you I don't!"

"I suppose you'd rather have the Vicar with her strap-on!"

Releasing his grip on her hip, he used his hand to guide his penis towards her vagina. Then, for the first time in more years than he could remember, he thrust his cock deep into her sex.

Nina clenched her teeth. She'd get her own back if it was the last thing she ever did...

***

Ali's black leather boots came up to her knees and had the highest, narrowest spiked heels that Leigh had ever seen, and her slicked back hair and harsh, outrageous make-up shouted of pent-up aggression.

Sitting at the back of the waiting room, the tight-fitting, black leather trousers pressed deliciously against Ali's mons squeezing against her pussy lips so that every movement rubbed the leather against them in an erotic caress. She'd teamed the trousers with an equally tight-fitting, black leather jacket worn zipped up to her neck to encase her in warm sensuality and beneath which she was naked.

Outwardly, she appeared cold and commanding, yet inside she was a cauldron of seething lust. She was only sorry she hadn't had time to thrash the adorable Cindy again. Surprised at the intensity of feeling the youngster had aroused within her, Ali knew she'd have to make a move on Leigh soon or go mad with wanting. Once, she'd missed the warmth and affection that only a lover can give but now her cold, sadistic nature grew stronger by the day. To watch skin turn red with the heat of humiliation sharpened her sexual appetite, and to hear sobs and screams as faces became contorted with pain had her chomping at the bit. Observing human flesh quiver beneath the lash was an absolute joy, the prelude to mind-blowing orgasms.

Ali gave an inward shrug; that's what comes of being brought up with tales of sadistic forebears, she guessed. While other children were put to bed with fairy tales of big bad wolves and gingerbread houses, Ali's bedtime stories had been about wicked Magistrate Maitland. Under the camouflage of upright citizenship that the law of the day provided him with, he'd tortured his opponents, along with the victims of his lust, in the specially equipped cellar of his manor house.

Of course, there'd always been a healthy supply of young virgins amongst their number, and the thought of the helpless girls twisting and writhing on his rack or undergoing a severe flogging sent bolts of electricity blazing through Ali's vagina.

Her lips curved into a tigerish smile; her eyes never left her prey with the voluminous, red-gold hair. Her thoughts hovered mistily between the erotic pleasure to be gained by seducing Leigh with kisses and the tantalizing notion of taming her by force. She knew she was treading on thin ice; if Leigh had even an inkling of what was on her mind, she'd flee in an instant.

***

9.45, and still no sign of Owen. Sitting at the desk behind the glass partition, Leigh scanned the battalion of scowling patients in the waiting room. If he didn't arrive soon, there'd be hell to pay.

She wasn't particularly anxious to see him again after his nocturnal visit, but the thought of postponing the meeting didn't exactly thrill her, either. She knew her own threats were useless; without Ali's leadership she'd never be vindictive enough to carry them through and destroy him. Nevertheless, he'd have no qualms about destroying her!

Without even a glance towards the back of the room, she knew Ali's dark, kohl lined eyes were upon her. Whatever Ali wanted, it certainly wasn't an appointment; she wasn't registered here as a patient. Leigh's hunch was that Ali was trying to work the old magic, win her over until she was so deeply under her spell that she'd do virtually anything asked of her. Just like the old days, when the girls were a force to be reckoned with. They'd never landed themselves in any real trouble, but it was more from good fortune than worthy intentions that they'd stayed on the right side of the law.

Leigh felt uneasy as the clanging of warning bells sounded in her head - Ali was looking for trouble. Like one of the big cats that stalk the forests at night, she was on the prowl. Ali had always had a mercurial nature and could switch from a joyful, relatively harmless mischief maker to an angry rebel in less than a heartbeat.

Yielding at last to the powerful, unspoken command, Leigh glanced up and met Ali's hot, relentless gaze. Sitting with her back straight and her arms folded across her chest, there was something deeply unnerving about Ali's presence in such innocuous surroundings; she was more dangerous than ever.

A patient exited Dr. Rankin's consulting room. Leigh checked the appointments book in front of her. But before she had time to call the next patient, Ali had set off down the hall towards Terence's room.

CHAPTER SEVEN

Dressed in a hideous, unflattering uniform, Claire Rankin looked up from the supermarket checkout. "Nina!"

"Good to see you, Claire." Nina felt better already as the warm fluttering in her stomach worked their way downward to her vagina. She'd been in a state of sexual agitation since that business with Owen at breakfast, though her feelings for him had been lukewarm for so long.

In a nervous gesture, Claire patted her immaculately styled, short, chestnut hair with her left hand. With a round face, she was pretty enough to get herself noticed; male customers always made a beeline for her checkout. While she'd be the first to admit she could do with losing a few pounds, as a mother of two grown-up children she was in pretty good shape. In an unconscious movement, she straightened her back and thrust out her pendulous breasts. The effect was pleasant enough, but not quite as she'd have liked.

"I haven't seen you for weeks, Nina. What are you doing here?" Her hand trembled ever so slightly as she took Nina's few items from the wire basket and passed them over the bar code scanner. "I thought we agreed you'd shop somewhere else? I can't talk here."

"I have to see you. What time do you get off work?"

"I've only been here an hour! Can't it wait?"

"Meet me in the Water Gardens in half an hour."

"How can I?" Claire hissed as she indicated the long queue that was already forming behind Nina.

"Be there." Nina indicated the long, thin implement wreathed in a silk scarf that stuck out from the top of her tote bag.

Terence smiled as the narrow waisted, leather-clad woman with the slicked back hair entered his consulting room. "It's good of you to come at such short notice." He was still smiling as she locked the door behind her.

He knew who she was, of course, having watched her grow up. And the memories were still ripe of the persistent bullying one of his sons had suffered at school. Never in his wildest dreams had Terence imagined that he'd one day make use of the services she now offered. Nor had he ever dreamed that such a small-boned, somewhat scrawny teenager would metamorphose into such a strikingly sensual young woman. Her heavily made-up eyes, like black coals in a red-hot fire, could burn a man to his very soul, and the scarlet-glossed lips were ripe for kissing.

He was still smiling. "For this first consultation."

"Shut up, you no good piece of chicken shit!" Despite her derogatory tone, Ali felt the stirrings of lust bubbling inside. "This is the first and last time you'll summon me. From now on, I give the orders. Got it?"

Terence's smile faded. "Well, y...yes, I suppose so, but..."

"But nothing. Stand up." She busied herself lighting a cigar.

"I'm sorry, but you can't smoke in here."

She lifted it to her lips and took a drag before blowing the smoke into his face. As a symbol of her authority, it would show him that she had a total disregard for the rules of convention.

"I don't like to repeat myself, Doctor."

Terence stood, all traces of good humour vanishing from his face to be replaced by quivering uncertainty. He fiddled with his glasses.

"Give me your belt - now!"

The hand she held out to him was small with long, slightly curved fingernails, painted black. He placed the belt across her palm and she coiled it tightly before slipping it into her pocket.

"Drop your trousers." Holding the cigar between her teeth, she stood with her hands on her hips as his trousers fell to the floor. "Now your pants."

Again, he obeyed her command without question. When he stood with trousers and pants around his ankles, again she held out her hand. He'd never know how much it excited her to reduce a man of his standing in the community to a pathetically gibbering idiot who would obey her every command. God, he looked so stupid! Clumsily hopping on first one leg, then the other, he extracted his feet and passed the garments to her, which she threw aside to land in a heap on the floor.

"I want you naked, apart from socks and shoes."

"Yes."

"My name's Mistress Blackheart. That's how you'll address me."

"Yes, Mistress Blackheart."

Ali gave a wintry smile. "You learn fast, Dr. Rankin." She waited until he stood before her, naked save for his tan coloured socks and shiny black shoes. "You look totally ridiculous, and are a particularly pathetic example of manhood."

Actually, he was in pretty good shape. Lean and athletic without an ounce of excess fat, he was smooth chested with fair, soft skin. There was a fine sprinkling of hair that covered his arms and legs, and a particularly thick crop of pubic hair, from which a modestly long but gloriously thick cock sprang up. If only she could relax her own rules, which precluded any fucking at all on a first appointment. She could feel her quim twitching with longing to suck in his powerful weaponry. Still, maybe next time...

Squaring her shoulders, as much to keep a reign on her own licentious enthusiasm as much as to gain control over him, she began the process of belittling him.

"Look at you! You're nothing but pasty skin, bone and hairy legs. Call that a cock? I've seen better than that on the end of a fishing rod." She cast a derisive eye over his upper body, where two defiant black hairs curled on an otherwise satin-skinned chest. She narrowed her eyes and gave a derisive laugh. "Don't tell me - that's one hair split down the middle."

With a sharp movement that reeked of pent-up aggression, she raked her fingers through her short, jet hair, scraping her scalp with her fingernails. She'd known Terence vaguely for many years but had never seen him as a potential fuck before.

Oh, to squeeze his cock witless with her vice-like pussy muscles. He was unaware that she still had dealings with one of his sons, who, having suffered from her bullying throughout adolescence, had been only too pleased to make use of her adult services now that she was back in town. And as Terence stood before her, she mentally compared the cocks of father and son, coming down very firmly in favour of the father's. Yes, if he played his cards right, she chuckled inwardly, Terence might just be in with a chance!

"Now, hands behind your back, wimp. Don't make a sound, or I'll have to gag you. Move away from the desk. Stand with your legs open and keep your eyes on the floor."

Transfixed, Terence watched the two slender fingers of one hand as they slid either side of the cigar. She removed it from her mouth and smoke billowed upward as she pursed her shiny red lips.

"Hurry up! You've got a waiting room full of patients."

His thick penis twitched, then twitched again. "Yes, Mistress Blackheart."

Obeying her commands, he cast his eyes downward and listened as she walked round behind him and unlocked the cupboard. He heard her rummage through the shelves, then walk back again. Standing behind him, she bound his wrists using some kind of surgical tape.

Unseen by Terence, Ali stubbed out the cigar on the glass of a framed photograph of a woman.

"Is this a picture of your wife?"

"Yes, Mistress."

"What a nice-looking woman."

Ali snatched up his stethoscope, then standing in front of him, she placed the ends in his ears before taping the round, metal end in position on his chest. His eager cock continued to rise to the occasion, ready for action. She gave his balls a hard squeeze.

"I thought you'd like to listen to the beating of your heart at the same time as I beat your arse." She took something from her pocket which she held beneath his lowered eyes. "Have you ever seen nipple clamps before? No? Well, here's how they work."

She took his tiny nipple between finger and thumb, relishing the acceleration of her excitement as his cock jerked, then pinched his nipple until it stood like a stiff peak. She opened the jaws of one clamp, and then closed it over the small, hard morsel. Her lips quivered at his sharp intake of breath as he experienced the pain of pleasure for the first time.

"As you see, it's joined by a chain to a second clamp, which is usually attached to the other nipple. But, seeing as how the stethoscope is in the way," she noted how he sighed with relief as she removed the clamp, "I thought we'd try something else. Put your tongue out and say 'ah."

As soon as he poked his tongue out, she snapped the clamp closed over it, then grabbed his rigid penis and squeezed it hard, relishing the way it throbbed.

"I thought I'd attach the other end...," using finger and thumb, she plucked at his foreskin, "here!"

His face contorted with agony and he cried out as the clamp pinched at the delicate area. He bent from the waist to try to relieve the tension. Quick as a flash, Ali snatched his belt from her pocket, flicked her wrist to uncurl it and struck him across the thigh.

"Aaaaah!"

"No, we've already done the 'say ah' bit. Be quiet, or someone will break the door down to see what's wrong. Unless, of course, you want your patients to see you like this? No, I thought not. Keep your bloody mouth shut and stand up straight."

With grim determination Terence pressed his lips together. His eyes glistened with moisture as the excruciating pain of the clamps bit in. He stood ramrod straight, his gaze focused on his penis.

Ali unzipped her jacket to let her firm, naked, upward-tilting breasts swing free.

"Look at my tits."

Terence looked, feasting and gorging himself senseless on the sight as she took each dark brown nipple, already hard and erect, and rolled them between finger and thumb.

"If you're a good boy and do as I say, I might let you suck them," she thrilled at the way his eager eyes bulged with lewd fascination, and his cock jerked upwards despite the pain, "but not today - we really mustn't keep your poor patients waiting much longer."

Holding the buckle end of the belt, she gave it a couple of turns round her hand and instructed, "face the wall."

When he'd taken up the required position, Ali stood behind him. She adjusted her own stance, then pulled back her hand. For a moment she concentrated, then with a satisfying Crack! of leather against bare flesh, she drew a wide line of red fire across his buttocks.

***

As she left the surgery, Ali glanced across to reception where one of the doctors was tearing Leigh off a strip in front of the whole waiting room. Blaming Leigh for the backlog caused by his own late arrival, and to some extent added to by Ali's liaison with her new client, he set about destroying Leigh's credibility in front of the patients.

Now, as she headed towards the car park, Ali reflected on the way her friend's pale complexion had turned an attractive shade of pink as humiliation washed over her. From her open-necked blouse to her hairline, her skin had positively glowed, making her look younger and more vulnerable than ever. The thought made Ali tremble with anticipation.

She unlocked the door of her shiny, yellow Ferrari and decided to head for the Water Gardens, an oasis of calm where the river passed through the town centre, a place to sit quietly and make her plans. Merely watching as the scene had unfolded behind the glass partition had made her own body heat rise by several degrees, and set her stomach muscles clenching and unclenching. Her nipples pushed against the leather of her jacket as she slid behind the wheel and gunned the engine.

Her hunger to join the Doctor in the humiliation of Leigh had been acute; yet she couldn't stand the thought that someone other than herself could cause such distress or have that degree of control over the girl she intended to dominate. Still, she'd set the ball rolling now; if things went according to plan she'd soon have Leigh exactly where she wanted her.

CHAPTER EIGHT

Sitting side by side on the bench overlooking the river, the two women embraced. Claire Rankin opened her mouth to allow entry to Nina's snaking tongue. They paid no attention to the pair of swans that glided effortlessly towards them in the hope of food scraps, nor the leather-clad woman sitting on the far bank, where the tots stood with their mothers throwing whole slices of bread to the waiting ducks.

Claire moaned as she felt the hand squeeze her breast. Breaking the kiss she said, "I told the Manager I had one of my migraines. I promised to do an extra shift on Saturday." She giggled. "I know I'm irresistible, Nina, but I thought we'd agreed to cool it for a while!" Claire rubbed her bottom as if it hurt. "Are you going to pick up where you left off?"

"That depends." Again, Nina indicated the scarf-sheathed implement, running her fingers up and down its length.

"On what?"

"Your co-operation."

Drawing the object from her bag slowly, Nina unwrapped the scarf to reveal a thin riding crop and ran it lovingly through her fingers. She raised it in the air, then with a Swish! brought it down against the side of the bench. The resulting Crack! drove away the swans and ducks in a commotion of feathers.

And on the far bank, Ali wondered where she'd seen the round faced, chestnut haired woman before.

Nina's own thrill at the sight of the crop matched Claire's, who drew back a couple of inches. The two women had been friends for several years, but had only become lovers a few months ago. Together they'd explored the emerging darker side of Nina's sexuality.

Although Nina loved to administer mild punishments with the crop, having discovered that domination over Claire brought about the best orgasms of her life, like the bondage they also enjoyed from time to time, it remained their secret. So far Nina hadn't tied up any of her other lovers or taken the crop to their backsides, though she fully recognized it was an itch that would one day have to be scratched.

"Ok Nina, what do you want?"

"You over there, behind that tree for starters," Nina pointed to an old, gnarled tree on the other side of a little clearing, "We'll discuss the other matters after I've given you a reminder of what the crop feels like."

"You're not going to do it here, in the open air?"

Nina put on the stern expression she usually saved for Owen. "That's for me to decide."

She took the other woman's hand and helped her to her feet. She picked up her tote bag and led Nina through the clearing and round behind the tree. Neither of them noticed that the woman in leather also rose from her bench and made for the little bridge that crossed the river, following at a discreet distance as Nina led her companion through the clearing and round behind the tree. Along with the surrounding vegetation, it proved to be an effective screen from passers by, and Nina couldn't help the tremble of excitement in her voice as she issued her orders.

"Pull your knickers down, then lean with your breasts against the trunk."

"What if we get caught?"

"We won't if you hurry up. Quickly."

With satisfying haste, Claire pulled her plain white panties down to her knees, then took a couple of awkward steps forward. Positioning her feet with her toes against the trunk, she clasped her hands in front of her eyes so as not to hurt her face on the bark as she rested her head against it. Then, with her breasts squashed flat against the trunk, Claire Rankin braced herself and waited for the impact.

When it came, it was like a blaze of fire across her generously proportioned rump. She couldn't help but scream.

"Shhh! Someone will hear you."

"I couldn't help it. You hit me too hard."

"Sorry." Except that she wasn't, Nina thought with a smile. Here in the open air, with people going about their daily business just a short distance away, her excitement was more intense than ever. To see Claire's pallid buttocks wobble as the livid red weal was raised was a delight that she just had to have more of. She raised the crop and brought it down heavily. Her aim wasn't perfect and the blow fell a little lower than she intended, catching Claire at an angle across the crease below the cheeks of her bottom.

"Please, Nina- no more! You're hurting me. Let's go home. Terence is at the surgery, so we'd have the house to ourselves. We could go to bed and talk."

Getting in the swing of things now, Nina brought the crop down hard. This time her aim was perfect, laying down a stripe over the first. Her clitoris throbbed in appreciation.

"We'll talk here. The thing is this..." she paused a moment, raised the crop, then added, "I think Owen's having an affair."

Claire turned her head to look at her. "So what? He's been having affairs ever since you got married."

"Eyes front!"

Nina brought the crop down, sadistically aiming to miss her mark and hitting the tree close to Claire's head instead. Oh, it was pure joy to see the terror in her friend's eyes, then watch that same terror drain away once the tree had absorbed what should have been Claire's pain.

"I've had enough. I want shot of him, want him out of my house. But he won't go... not unless I can make him see that it would be better for him if he did. I'm convinced his latest trollop is a patient, and I want to get a job at the surgery, as a receptionist. That way I can find out who she is. Then I can confront him with the evidence and threaten to shop him to the authorities if he doesn't get out."

"Why tell me? Talk to Owen."

"He'd never agree."

"I don't see what I can do." Claire stuffed her hand in her mouth to stifle a cry as Nina's crop came crashing down again.

"I want you to talk to Terence - Owen might listen to him."

***

"Come," Owen said when Leigh knocked on the door. Already seated at his desk, without lifting his eyes from the notes in front of him, he used a hand gesture to order her to take up a position beside him. "On your knees. You know what I want."

The man was unbelievable! "You've only just got here, and there's a waiting room full of people!"

"Do it," he swivelled round in his chair to face her, "or get out there and tell them to go home; that surgery's cancelled. It's up to you."

She was lucky to have come through the ugly scene that had just taken place unscathed; to break such news now to a room full of angry people whose sympathies could switch back and forth in a moment was asking for trouble.

Besides, there was still that annoying irritation that needed to be eased - she wanted his cock in her mouth as much as he did.

Pushing all thoughts about the unfairness of it all to the back of her mind, she lowered herself to her knees while Owen opened his legs to give her access. With one hand holding his leg, she reached for the hasp of the zip and, with trembling fingers, unfastened his trousers and extracted his already erect penis from his boxer shorts. Oh, how she hated those things!

Despite everything that had gone before, she felt the quickening of her pulses as she took his velvety glans between her lips. She flicked out her tongue and poked it into the tiny slit, which was already leaking salty fluid. When he groaned, she slipped a hand beneath his scrotum and, caressing his balls gently, took his cock right into the warmth of her mouth and began to suck.

As much as she hated him, and it was true- she really did hate him - she couldn't help the spirals of heat that spread from her loins to her tightening breasts. By now she was completely hooked on the joys of cock-teasing. The downside was, and probably always would be, that the actual act of fucking never turned out to be as great as she'd anticipated. It was probably her own fault, she told herself, for letting her wantonness build the act up to some great earth-shattering event. She was still waiting for the toe curling and the fireworks.

"It's time to renegotiate your terms of employment", Owen told her between ragged gasps. "Further to our previous agreement, not to mention your scurrilous threats, if you want to continue working in this town, you'll keep your mouth shut about the cock-ups this morning. I intend to protect my interests and those of my colleagues by any means available. I've no intention of appearing incompetent, nor do I want to find myself hauled up before the authorities for anything that may, or may not, take place within these walls." He laughed. "Or anywhere else. So, in the future, you'll take the blame for everything- and I do mean everything- that goes wrong."

Heat rose in his balls as she manipulated them. She took his cock deeper into her warm, wet mouth, making slurping noises that were enough to drive him insane. She knew he was having trouble controlling himself, and that was just the way she liked it. However, the fact remained that he had the upper hand.

Tiny beads of sweat formed on Owen's forehead as he tried to keep an even tone under her delicious ministrations.

"I want you 'on call' twenty four hours a day. Of course, I'll see that you receive benefits appropriate to your new position. If, however, you fail to comply with any of my demands, I'll have you named and shamed in the local press."

Horror-stricken, she pulled away sharply and his cock was rudely expelled.

"For what?" she demanded sitting back on her heels

"Oh, I'll think of something, we all have secrets. And a man in my position is always believed over the likes of someone with your reputation. And if I were you, I wouldn't want anyone delving too deeply into my background." Seeing her puzzled expression, he expanded. "I've done my homework, Leigh. You've been quite active in this town - you were a bit of a hell raiser as a teenager, and now you're a slut, like your mother before you. Don't look so shocked - the whole town had her, including me! Now get out, and send in the first of my patients."

He waited until she reached the door, and then called after her. "Make yourself available directly after this morning's surgery."

***

Things were going great. Leigh had taken the bait, and Ali opened the door to her wearing high, strappy stiletto heeled shoes and long, black gloves that came up to her armpits.

"I'm sorry to call unannounced..." Leigh began.

Riverside Tower's security desk was equipped with a bank of monitors. Far from being unannounced, the guard had tipped Ali off to Leigh's arrival more than three minutes before.

"If you're expecting visitors," Leigh gaped at Ali's dress, so tight she must have been poured into it, "I won't stay long. It's just that there was a bit of bother at the surgery this morning and I need a shoulder to cry on."

Speaking of shoulders, it stuck Leigh that Ali's off-the-shoulder neckline seemed in some confusion as to where her neck actually was. Cut diagonally, it started beneath her right armpit and sliced across her left breast, which was recklessly balanced and held in place by willpower alone. It looked wonderful on Ali, and in her dreams Leigh wore one just like it.

In her dreams - huh! The story of her life.

Ali stood back to let Leigh pass. "You're welcome anytime." If there was one thing Ali could count on, it was Leigh's curiosity. It must have driven her mad wondering why she'd turned up at the surgery to see Terence, only to leave again without a word. Now all she had to do was spring the trap.

Leigh stepped dazedly into the apartment and followed Ali. Several closed doors led off from the hall, with more leading off from the spacious lounge in which she found herself. "Wow! It's some place you've got here."

"It's home," Ali said modestly.

"Yeah, sure - a bit more up-market than the terraced house you grew up in, right?"

Normally, Leigh would be too polite to pry but she'd never believed Ali's schoolgirl boasts about having come from a wealthy background. Now she was curious as to how Ali could afford to live in one of the most expensive properties for miles around.

"You must have made some useful contacts in Europe."

Ali smiled at the generosity of Chantel and some of the chateau's guests who, on the understanding that they'd always find a welcome at Ali's establishment should they ever have business in the City, had put up considerable sums. Without their help she'd have had to settle for something more modest, without the benefits of the tight security.

Leigh's gaze took in the spotless, unlived-in appearance of her surroundings. "And you must have a whole army of char ladies to keep the place this spotless." She remembered the un-cared for clutter of Ali's old bedroom, and the way Ali used to stick chewing gum under tables or on the back of bus seats; the way she'd just chuck coke cans, or more usually beer cans, over her shoulder for some other poor sod to clear away.

"Not at all," Ali flicked her eyes towards the kitchen and smiled a secret smile. "Though I have got someone who 'does' for me. But that's enough about my domestic arrangements." She wasn't sure what the story was with the doctor, but things couldn't have worked out better. "Go and sit down. I just have to check on something, then I'll be with you in a minute and you can tell me what's wrong."

"Sorry. Have I called at a bad time?"

"Of course not! Have you eaten?"

"No. I came straight from evening surgery."

"You wait here, and I'll rustle something up."

Ali disappeared through one of the doors. The glorious aromas that were already emanating from the room beyond suggested that Ali's culinary skills had also improved considerably and that "rustling something up" had a completely different meaning here.

Leigh swept her eyes over the lounge. While she tended to favour the traditional warmth of oak beams and chintz rather than the cold elegance preferred by Ali, she recognized quality when she saw it. Decked out in stylish black wood and smoked glass, the severe feel of the room was relieved by a couple of large, bronze figurines, both nudes Leigh noticed. There was also some kind of tall, spreading plant standing in the corner, and one of the chairs had over-stuffed, out-of-place, leopard print cushions.

The kitchen door opened - and to her dismay, Leigh heard Ali's harsh whispers. Oh Lord! Her visitors were here already.

"Look, Ali, if you've got company, I can always come back some other time."

"I'm expecting John later." Seeing Leigh's puzzled look, Ali elaborated. "You know, John Micklem, from the pub?"

"Oh, I'd forgotten about him. You don't think he'll really turn up?"

Ali took a seat beside Leigh on the sofa. "Of course he'll fucking turn up! Men like him always do. We've got about an hour before he gets here. Until then, there's only you, me and Jurgen."

"Who's Jur...?"

"No one important." Ali's tone was dismissive, but the intensity of passion in her eyes told a very different story indeed, one that Leigh was quick to pick up on.

"You didn't tell me you'd come back from Europe with a lover," Leigh laughed, her voice the familiar tinkle that re-awakened her friend's hunger.

"He's not my lover! He just cleans and cooks for me." Ali's glossed, crimson lips were a thin line of contempt.

The door opened and Leigh's hand flew to cover her mouth as Jurgen entered. Well over six feet, he was handsome and tanned - Hercules himself would envy Jurgen's pecks! And Leigh wanted him, whether he was Ali's lover or not. The man was truly gorgeous, a walking representation of perfect manhood - the kind of guy you see pictures of but never get to meet.

Not only that - he was stark naked save for a black bow tie!

"What do you want?" Ali snapped as he approached.

"Dinner's ready, Mistress. Shall I serve?"

Leigh's mouth dropped open. What was this "Mistress" rubbish?

"No. Stand there," Ali instructed curtly, pointing to a spot in front of where the two friends were seated. "Stand straight, man. Head bowed, legs apart, hands behind your back."

Thrilled by Leigh's shocked intake of breath, Ali fought to suppress a smile as she waited for Jurgen to comply. Rising to her feet, she walked round behind him and, producing a length of her favoured cord, bound his wrists together before re-taking her seat.

"My friend wants to examine you."

Leigh's heart thudded in the back of her throat, and her words came out as a high-pitched, "I what?"

"Go on," Ali encouraged, "he doesn't bite." When Leigh remained seated, Ali said "You want to be examined like a horse in a sale, don't you, Jurgen?"

"Yes, Mistress."

"Ali, I can't!"

"Yes you can! Don't mind him. He's nothing but a shit. What are you, Jurgen?"

"A shit, Mistress."

"A shit with a shrivelled banana where his cock should be." Ali felt the hot surge of power pound through her veins. "Tell the lady what you are."

"A shit with a shrivelled banana where my cock should be."

"See, he's a wimp," Ali felt a bolt of liquid fire shoot through her as Jurgen's cock stirred, "too weak to argue." Oh, it really was the most magnificent organ on the planet - not that she'd ever admit that to him. "Go on, Leigh. Imagine you're buying him and want to check he's worth the asking price."

Slowly, Leigh got to her feet. Momentarily transfixed by the sexiest, most imposing male specimen she'd ever set eyes on, she struggled vainly to make sense of the situation. Something didn't sit right- there was something going on here that she didn't understand; he was a man who could have any girl he wanted, yet he seemed totally dominated by Ali, a woman who's head came up to his armpits and seemed to get off on humiliating him.

Gingerly, Leigh touched the tips of her trembling fingers against his tight chest, then skidded them downward. The response to her soft touch was immediate; his penis shot up hard and rigid from his groin and, at the same time sent unbearably hot, throbbing desire straight to her clit.

CHAPTER NINE

Taking up her characteristically majestic pose with her forearms resting on the arms of her favourite chair, Ali perused the pair side-on. They made a rather attractive couple - perhaps too attractive? No, she had no worries there; she could control Jurgen. Besides, manipulating people always made her horny, and Leigh was as easy to manipulate now as she'd always been.

"What do you think of him?" Ali demanded. "Come on, truth or forfeit."

Leigh giggled. "Oh no! I've paid you enough forfeits to last a lifetime!" Leigh rested her hands on Jurgen's hips and drew in a breath. With her head coquettishly on one side, she swayed her hips provocatively. "How can you call him a wimp? He's magnificent!"

"You want proof? Ok, do what the fuck you want to him. Tease him as much as you like, but I guarantee he won't move unless I allow it." Seeing the doubtful look on her friend's face, Ali laughed, and in an echo of former times, dared her.

Leigh kicked off her shoes. Taking up the challenge, with a flirtatious smile she began to gyrate her hips sensuously, every now and then thrusting her abdomen forward in blatant invitation. Slowly, she unbuttoned her blouse.

Jurgen's head remained bowed and his eyes stayed fixed to the floor.

Ali settled more comfortably. She knew he'd be going through hell as he tried to ignore the enticing movements of Leigh. After all, she was having trouble herself. It was she, Ali, who'd taught Leigh the movements, but now Leigh surpassed her teacher in that department. She was a true wanton, and had the makings of a perfect sex slave.

Leigh wet her lips, and then threw back her head so that her carefully styled, disorderly bedroom-hair tumbled about her shoulders. Then, in the way she'd perfected in her quest to tease every member of the male species, she began a sexy striptease until she stood naked before him. But only the twitching of his huge, erect phallus proved that he was a living, breathing man.

A rush of electricity scorched Ali's insides. When she'd first seen Leigh in the pub, she'd recognized at once the blossoming of her friend's body, but nothing had prepared her for the delight that stood before her. Even Jurgen's huge hands would find it hard to contain the cherry-tipped breasts.

Her narrow waist seemed all the more so due to those firm, juicily heavy globes and the sensuous flare of her hips. Her pert backside was deliciously fleshy, and Ali's insides quivered even more at the thought of sinking her fingers deep into the furrow that separated her buttocks.

Leigh danced for Jurgen, erotically twirling and swaying like some exotic dancer in a nightclub. Her jiggling breasts slapped against each other as she kicked her extraordinary long, pale legs high in front of him. There was nothing she liked more than displaying her body for a man when he was unable to respond, and she was really turned on now. She was blisteringly hot both inside and out, and little beads of perspiration formed on her skin to trickle tantalizingly down the deep valley between her breasts.

Ali noticed them too, though only the slight tremble of her hands gave an indication of her feelings as she swung her eyes up and down, left and right, in an effort to drink in the heady sight of both glorious bodies. Even now she wasn't entirely sure who she wanted the most, well hung Jurgen or the delectable Leigh.

Leigh however was beginning to tire of the game. She wanted Jurgen more than she'd ever wanted a man before, and she wanted him now. But he remained stubbornly impassive and, admitting defeat at last, Leigh stopped her dancing and came to a halt to stand facing him.

Ali was triumphant. "I told you he wouldn't do anything! You're not man enough, are you?" Her satin voice was nevertheless caustic as she speared him with a cold glance.

"No, Mistress."

An unthinkable possibility hit Leigh's brain like a ten-ton lorry. "You mean he's..." she broke off and looked quizzically at the hard, twitching penis. Surely not! Turning to face Ali, she took a couple of steps closer and lowered her voice to a conspiratorial whisper. "He's gay? What a waste to womankind!"

For the first time Leigh noticed Ali had something lying across her lap - surely it wasn't what it looked like, because what it looked like was a riding crop. It probably wasn't a good idea to question its purpose. Something akin to panic fluttered in her depths

Ali laughed, but didn't lower her own voice as she announced acidly, "Of course he's not gay! Look at him! He wants to fuck you so much he's about to bust his gut. Tell the lady what you want, Jurgen."

Without raising his head, he said "I want to fuck you, Lady."

Now Ali was really enjoying herself. "You want to fondle her wonderfully succulent tits, and take her hard nipples into your mouth, don't you, Jurgen?"

"Yes, Mistress."

"You want to fuck us both, don't you, wimp?"

His next words came out as a strangled sound from deep in his throat. "I want to fuck the arse off you both, you black hearted bitch!"

Crack!

It was Leigh who yelled out as the crop caught Jurgen across his buttocks. Jurgen, however didn't even flinch but merely stood his ground as Ali degraded him further.

"Shut the fuck up! That pathetic attachment between your legs isn't worthy to flaunt itself, let alone fuck such juicy pussies. Still, since we have a few moments to spare, the Lady will give you a blow job." Thrilling at Leigh's horrified gaze, Ali felt her blood surge in a fiery tide through her veins. She commanded harshly "Leigh, suck him!"

Not entirely averse to taking advantage of such an abnormal situation, Leigh thought it seemed impolite, not to mention chancy, to refuse her hostess when she was in this mood. She dropped to her knees in front of him. Her nipples, surrounded by dark areolae, stood out firm and ripe. Hungrily, she reached out for his balls. Cupping them in her hands, she flicked out her tongue and swirled it over his velvet-headed penis.

Enjoying herself immensely, for some minutes Leigh continued to flick her tongue over his glans, shiny from his secretions, and relished the slightly salty taste on her tongue. Clutching his massive cock with one hand she stroked his scrotum with the other. Then, holding his thigh to steady herself, she flicked her tongue downwards, slowly tracing the rope-like vein.

Repositioning herself, she eased her head between his legs and explored his balls with the very tip of her tongue.

Leigh almost jumped a foot in the air as the Crack! broke the silence of the room and Ali brought the crop down against the side of the chair. Her smooth, satin voice with the edge of steel was full of menace.

"Suck him, you stupid little tart! You're supposed to be giving him a blow job, not auditioning for the Olympic Testicle Tickling team!"

Leigh barely had time to react before Ali was on her feet. Clutching a handful of the soft, red-gold hair, she yanked back Leigh's head.

Leigh let out a shriek as she knelt before the statue-like Jurgen. "For God's sake, Ali! That hurt."

"Hurt?" Still clutching a fistful of hair, Ali pulled Leigh's head forward again, into the required position. "You don't know the meaning of the word. Open your mouth." Letting Leigh's hair drop, she grabbed Jurgen's cock and rammed it half way down Leigh's throat, making her gag terribly. "Get on with it!" There was a swishing sound, followed by a Crack! as Ali's crop came down. A flash of fire streaked across Leigh's shoulder blades, and she almost choked as the tumescent flesh stifled her scream. Immediately, her hand flew up behind her to soothe it. At once, the crop crashed down over her hand.

"Now that probably did hurt," Ali laughed, a knot of excitement tangling in her belly. "I won't put up with arguments, especially from you."

Sucking now for all she was worth, Leigh flicked her eyes upward to meet Ali's and saw the cruel smile that twisted her crimson lips.

"You can do better than that, Slut! Hurry up! We haven't eaten yet, and John will be here any minute." She raised the crop, fighting the urge to beat her friend as harshly as she'd beaten Cindy. "Suck him as if your life - or at the very least, your soft, unblemished skin - depended on it."

Leigh didn't know whether it was fear or arousal that made her tremble, but as she took Jurgen's thick, stiff shaft even deeper into her throat, her heart sang. There was something thrilling about being here like this, under threat of pain while sucking the huge erection of a man who'd surrendered himself completely to the will of another woman. It was so exciting, so wrong... yet felt so right.

Another line of fire blazed across her back; Jurgen yelled out as the shock forced Leigh's teeth to close around his flesh. Almost immediately, she felt her muscles go into spasm. No, don't let her come yet! She felt achingly alive. Oh, it was just so delicious. No! Please don't let her come yet.

Too late!

The full force of a mighty orgasm hit, sending shock waves right to her toes, and the fireworks she craved really did light up her brain.

At the same moment, Jurgen's body jerked violently. A strangled growl escaped his lips as his hot seed shot into her mouth. Leigh almost choked a second time, yet she daren't eject his cock without being told to.

Ali's voice dripped sarcasm as she untied Jurgen's hands.

"When you've quite finished, Leigh, go through to the dining room. Jurgen, it's time you served dinner."

***

Complacent in the knowledge that John Micklem would be livid at being kept waiting for so long, especially if he'd gone to a lot of trouble to arrange cover at the pub, Ali smiled. No doubt he'd be working on a little speech while under the perceptive eye of the security guard, and would find the innuendo in the guard's look most disconcerting when he realized the guard was privy to some kind of knowledge he didn't have.

At last Ali relented and rang down to the desk. If she could have seen it she'd have been pleased with the wide-eyed nod of the guard's head and the broad, mocking grin with which he informed John he could finally go up to her apartment.

On opening the door, she knew instantly that he was shaken by her formidable presence; her very being oozed a dark sexuality that set his cock twitching. She guessed he didn't feel half as confident as his brave words suggested.

"I don't know who the hell you are, lady," he began in a woefully unsuccessful bid to gain the upper hand, "but you'd better make this worth my while. I don't like being messed about. We both know what you want, so lead the way to the bedroom."

Wordlessly, she ushered him into the sitting room with a look that made him feel rather foolish. He looked her over from her dark, heavily made-up eyes down to her high-heeled shoes that brought her height up to his. He took in the long black gloves, and then feasted his eyes greedily on the swell of her left breast. Balanced precariously, it was almost completely visible as the dress sliced across it.

Momentarily at a loss, he gave her a quick smile that she didn't return. In a flash of bravado he reached out to touch her, but seemed to decide against it and let his hand drop to his side. And she could almost hear the cogs turning as he racked his brains for something clever to say, to try a different tack. He'd probably draw on his years of experience as a pub landlord.

True to form, his mouth broke into the leering smile he saved for his young, female customers.

"You're a real traffic-stopper, Darlin', that's for sure."

Unimpressed by what was obviously his favoured chat-up line, Ali instructed crisply, "take your clothes off." His lust was so intense she could smell it.

"Okaaaaay," he dragged the word out in the mistaken belief it sounded sexy, "down to business. I like that in a woman."

CHAPTER TEN

The door was ajar. Sitting in the kitchen where Ali had instructed her to "stay put and keep quiet," Leigh thought over the bizarre events of the evening. Clearly, far from being unannounced, she'd been expected.

Insisting that Leigh remain naked while they ate, Ali had made no reference to what had gone before, while Jurgen served them with a delicious meal of beef braised in brandy as if it was just a normal day at the office.

Even so, Leigh wished she'd told Ali about Owen, but after this evening she wasn't sure she could trust her. She'd been hurt emotionally as well as physically by Ali's crop. But what worried her most was that it had induced such an intense reaction.

Jurgen hadn't joined them at the table but was on hand to keep their glasses topped up. Leigh was no expert on wine but a cursory glance at the label confirmed that a bottle of this stuff would cost her more than a week's wages. Still, Ali had always had expensive tastes.

The dessert had been a heavenly concoction of strawberries, chocolate, cream and some kind of liqueur.

Feeling light-headed, Leigh peered through the gap into the lounge, confident that she could watch the proceedings without being seen. And watch she did - with a tissue stuffed in her mouth to stifle her giggles.

Ali's eyes swept over John's naked, pasty, inadequately maintained body. Obviously the only exercise he'd done of late was walk the hundred or so yards from the pub to Ali's apartment block. Sadly, gravity had worked its magic; freed from restraining clothing, John's oversized belly sagged towards the floor.

"When did you last see your tackle?" Ali arched a mocking eyebrow.

"Now listen here! I didn't come here to be insulted!"

"Really, John," the humiliation in his eyes brought the glitter of sadistic delight to Ali's, "you're far too sensitive!"

She reached for his insignificant penis with her gloved hand. Once again, her zest for power triggered fiery sparks of arousal. Few men realized just how vulnerable they were when naked. And these first few moments, when she could make or break a man, always turned her on.

However, she was pleasantly surprised when, after only a moment of gentle coaxing, his phallus had mushroomed to quite an acceptable size.

Releasing her hold, she commanded acidly, "sit!"

"What's this?" he gave a nervous laugh, "some sort of playground game? You tell me to skip, and I skip. You tell me to put my hands on my head, and..."

Ali's voice exploded like a firecracker. "Sit! You'll do as you're told or get the bloody hell out of my face!"

Huffily, John sat on the floor in the middle of the room, his legs stretched out before him.

"Open your legs."

He seemed to grasp now that in this weird, highly charged atmosphere he was completely out of his depth and obeyed without further question. Yet his cock throbbed visibly in anticipation as he looked longingly up at her.

Ali stood between his outstretched legs. She was aggressive, heartless and seductive, and he knew he'd never met anyone like her before. And judging by the look in his eyes, the poor creature had thought of little else but fucking her since he'd first set eyes on her days ago when she'd degraded him in his own pub.

"You mean less to me than a fly on a pile of dog shit," she told him as she brushed imaginary flecks of dust off her outstretched, black-gloved arm. It was about now, Ali thought, that heat would flood into his balls and, when she was sure his attention was centred on her ineffectual gesture, she delivered a swift, vicious kick to his crotch.

He yowled like a wounded pig as agony had him doubling over his middle-age spread, clutching his balls protectively.

At once, heat rampaged through Ali's veins. She was alive, and her vagina clenched in acknowledgement. There was something about dishing out pain that made her heart sing. Instinctively, she flicked her eyes towards the kitchen door, where the delectable Leigh watched silently.

"Cruel bitch!" he yelled.

"Exactly!" Ali's mouth quirked. "Now we understand each other. Did you bring the items I requested?"

"In my pocket," he said, sullenly.

Momentarily turning her back, Ali extracted the dog collar and lead from his jacket pocket. She took up her former position and admired the tan leather briefly.

"Good quality."

She grabbed his hair. He made no objection as she pulled his head forward to buckle the collar around his neck.

"Who's a good doggie, then?" she crooned, patting his head. She extracted her breasts from the dress with her gloved hands. "Has Mumsy-wumsy got something nice for the little doggie?"

His head snapped upright, his eyes ogling the ripe, up-tilting breasts that she offered him. The sight of the malleable, soft flesh against the black gloves was too much for him and he leapt to his feet. Instantly, she dealt a brutal slap to his cheek.

"Bad doggie!" She kicked his feet from under him, making him topple awkwardly. "On your knees! If you want a treat you'll have to beg."

Eager to fill his mouth with her glorious orbs, John found himself obeying. With his knees bent beneath him, he pulled his arms into his chest and let his hands flop forward in the classic begging position of a pooch. For added effect, he widened his eyes and stuck out his slavering tongue, panting loudly.

Ali leaned forward. She pulled his head forward once more and stuffed her right breast into his slobbering mouth. Immediately, he began sucking noisily, his saliva coating her flesh and forming little strings. His fingers reached out and closed around the hardened nipple of her other breast. Twirling with one hand and with his mouth full of glorious tit, he must have thought he was in heaven.

"Enough!" she said stepping backward so abruptly that he fell forward.

He threw out his arms and found himself on all fours. As he looked up at her, she pushed her slashed neckline down to her waist and flaunted her breasts with such an obvious delight that his saliva trickled down his chin. She turned the collar so that the buckle and small ring were at the front, then produced a shiny disc and held it out for his inspection.

"I've had it engraved. Read it to me."

"Bloody hell!" he said in an undertone that was a strange blend of pride and humiliation. He read the words as confidently as he was able. "Mongrel. Return to Mistress Blackheart."

"Good dog." Again, she patted his head. "You're to wear the collar every time you visit me," she told him, fixing the disc to the ring at the front," and you will visit me again - often. You'll come to need your fix of degradation as much as you long to fuck me." She clipped the lead to the ring. "I might just pop into the pub from time to time. When that happens, you're to produce the collar and fasten it round your neck. Or better still, you can keep it on - yes, keep it on and wear it all the time. That way, I won't have to punish you if I catch you without it."

"How can I? People will see."

"Then you'd better start wearing turtle necks."

With a terse command she summoned Jurgen, who immediately appeared from a side door with a dog bowl and a bottle of Dom Perignon.

John's penis shrivelled with humiliation at the sight of the big man, whose cock was far larger than his even when flaccid.

Jurgen put the bowl on the floor in the corner of the room, then walked across to the drinks cabinet and found two champagne flutes. He filled these with the sparkling liquid, then handed one to Ali before crossing to the kitchen.

In a rare moment of intimacy, he smiled down at Leigh as he handed her the filled flute. She smiled back as she accepted it.

Jurgen returned to the sitting room, and Leigh's curiosity was aroused when he took a small, black, unmarked bottle from the cabinet and proceeded to fill the dog bowl with thick, brown liquid. Afterwards, he disappeared through the door from which he'd come.

Ali gave a jerk on the lead and made John follow her on all fours. With the top of her dress pushed down to her waist, her breasts swung temptingly as she led him round in a circle. She gave another jerk on the lead and led him round the furniture a couple of times, had him pretend to cock his leg against the plant, then made him crawl across to the bowl where she commanded him to drink.

He lapped at it cautiously, then spat it back into the bowl.

"I can't drink that! It's disgusting."

Ali jerked his head upward, at the same time delivering another brutal kick, this time to his ribs.

"Shut your ugly mouth!" Knowing that no matter how much he complained, he was in a state of high sexual agitation, she threatened him. "If you want to stay, you'll drink the bowl dry. Otherwise, you get the fuck out of here. What's it to be?"

Reluctantly, he lowered his head, and began to lap at the foul-tasting liquid once more.

Flicking her eyes across to the kitchen doorway, Ali read the silent question on Leigh's lips. For a fleeting moment, Ali's mischievous smile was like that of a much younger, less treacherous Ali as she mouthed the answer.

"Gin, diet cola and brown sauce."

***

After allowing John a short rest, Ali had him kneel, then made him sit back on his legs.

"Rest that lazy arse on your ankles." She kicked out at his legs, encouraging him to hurry. "I'm the hardest bitch you'll ever kneel before!" When she was satisfied with the result, she walked around behind him, instructing him not to turn round.

"Stay there. Understand?"

John nodded, and received another kick, this time to his buttocks. "Now do you understand?"

"Yes."

"Yes, Mistress Blackheart," she corrected. "We'll try it again, and this time you'd better get it right."

Spirals of excitement coiled upward from her pulsating clitoris to her nipples as his saggy flesh trembled. Now he was really afraid of her; could Magistrate Maitland ever have felt as alive as she felt now? What she'd give to have his mansion, complete with its dark, airless dungeon, crammed full with its torture equipment, at her disposal. Sadly, it had suffered after his death and the estate had virtually fallen into ruins. Salvation for the old place had come in the guise of property developers. They'd moved in some years ago and turned the place into a country club.

Ali sighed. She'd just have to make do with the apartment. But when the funds were in place, she'd expand to the floor below. Of course, to raise the kind of cash required, she'd have to take on the training of more slaves like Cindy...

She came out of her reverie. "Do you understand, you spineless toad?" she snapped

"Yes, Mistress Blackheart" His voice was barely audible.

"Louder!"

"Yes, Mistress Blackheart!"

Black-browed and belligerent, she replied bitingly, "at last! For a moment I thought I had a complete idiot on my hands. Listen, you worthless pile of shit, I demand obedience from my slaves, and have some rather unpleasant ways of dealing with indiscipline that I can't wait to try out!"

With that, she left the room and tense moments passed. When she returned, the watching Leigh once again had to stuff a tissue in her mouth to stifle her reactions, as disbelief and curiosity jostled for dominance. For not only was Ali carrying a couple of metal poles but the elegant evening dress had gone, along with the gloves and shoes.

Her intimidating black leather waspie extended from just below her breasts to her hips and fastened with wide straps across the front. Ali loved the restrictions and fastened the silver buckles as tightly as she was able, drawing in further her already narrow waist. Round her long, graceful neck, she too wore a collar; wide enough to keep her head upright, it was decorated with silver studs, as were the long, leather gauntlets that replaced her gloves. Her impossibly high platform boots with spiky heels were also decorated with studs and buckled from her ankle right up to her shapely thighs.

Her stiff, dark nipples betrayed the depth of her arousal as they stood out like bullets from her naked breasts. She wasn't wearing panties and her labia, already glistening with her juices, hung red and inviting beneath the black rug of wiry curls that adorned her mons.

For some reason, Leigh's own thighs ached to spread themselves wide. The tousle-haired redhead allowed herself an indulgent smile and relished the strange swell of pride she felt at being privileged to observe the hot sensuality of Ali's body. Then, ashamed to even think such a thing, she covered her face with her hands. Her splintering breath was hot against her palms and she swallowed hard, turning her attention back to the unfolding scene in the sitting room.

Once again standing behind the obediently immobile John, Ali fixed leather restraints to each of his ankles. Then she fixed a metal spreader bar, about the girth of a broom handle, between his ankles using the hooks at each end to attach to the restraints. Next, she took a similar bar and, turning his collar so that the ring was at the back, she unclipped the lead which she threw aside. In its place, she clipped one end of the bar, similarly fixing the other end to a hook set in the centre of the spreader bar.

Lastly, she drew his hands behind his back and handcuffed his wrists together over the cruel bar that kept his back straight.

She eyed him with sadistic delight as she circled him a couple of times, finally stopping in front of him. Her skin tingled as a torrid warmth spread through her at the thought of Leigh similarly restrained; she'd have to slake her appetite soon, but on the other hand she hated to deny herself the joy of anticipation.

John's eyes brimmed with anxiety, and something else, too, something which looked very much like lust. And who could blame him when the object of his desire stood before him, like a demon in black leather? His cock reared up in front of him, once again hard and ready for action.

"Do you want to fuck me, John?"

"Yes, you crazy bitch!"

There was a loud Smack! Smack! as her hand made contact first with one cheek then the other.

"Yes what?"

"Yes, Mistress Blackheart."

She flicked her eyes towards the kitchen. "Leigh. Get in here, now!"

Ali savoured the look of horror-stricken recognition on John's face as the lovely young woman stepped naked into the room and approached him. On Ali's instruction, Leigh went through to Ali's bedroom and returned with the item she found lying on the bed, secretly wishing it were Owen and not John who was suffering at Ali's hands.

She handed the object to Ali. As she obeyed Ali's command and settled herself on the sofa, Ali held the object up for Leigh to see. It was black, and at first glance Leigh thought it was a sink plunger, with a slightly smaller than usual rubber section to fit over the plug hole. But to her surprise a closer inspection revealed it to be a dildo that resembled a fully erect penis. Perfect in every detail, Leigh could see now that the plunger part was in fact a hollow base that flared out like replica balls, to which straps were fitted.

Ali placed the base over John's nose, which fitted snugly into the hollow and left his mouth free to breathe. His startled eyes looked out over it as she buckled it around his head. With hands on hips she stood back to admire her work.

"Bloody hell, John, what a huge weapon!" Her dark eyes glittered as she laughed. "So," towering above him in her platforms, she stood with her legs either side of his head and her boots pressing firmly against his legs, "fuck me."

Lowering herself and using her hands, she guided the dildo into position and nudged it against her sensitive, glistening pussy lips. Grinning wickedly, she parted them with her fingers and then drove her quim downward, impaling herself onto the rigid phallus. Her heart thudded as a surge of power erupted into a maniacal laugh. He was helpless to do anything other than watch as she ground down madly, her breasts swinging and her mons hitting his chin.

Swept away in a frenzy of lust and power, Ali ground hard against the dildo. As her fervour increased, so to did the speed of her up and down movements. She reached down and sought out the hard nub of her clitoris and, rubbing it for all she was worth, brought herself ever closer to her moment of release.

When Jurgen entered the room at her command, with an almost imperceptible nod of her head she gave him the pre-arranged signal. He helped Leigh to her feet before guiding her towards his mistress, then positioned her to stand beside John with her back to Ali. Taking his place in front of her he widened his legs to bring himself closer to her height. With an encouraging smile, he made to part her thighs with his hand.

Leigh didn't need any encouragement, her thighs opened of their own volition. She was already wet and accepted the bulbous head of Jurgen's cock hungrily as it nudged her labia open.

Then, with one glorious, powerful thrust he entered her, burying his shaft up to the hilt inside the welcoming, moist warmth of her vagina. His huge hands gripped her waist tightly, rooting her to the spot.

He needn't have worried, she had no intention of going anywhere.

Having longed all evening to feel him throbbing inside her, she closed her eyes and melted into the moment, letting the sensual waves wash over her. Warm and contented, she was only vaguely aware of the arm that came round the front of her head.

She caught the smell of leather from Ali's gauntlet as fingernails gently scraped her lips. Parting them automatically to admit the finger, Leigh began to suck it as if it were a second penis rather than her best friend's probing digit, and felt a moment of abandonment when Ali withdrew it, glistening with Leigh's saliva.

Leigh tensed suddenly and her eyes flew open as she felt Ali's nail scrape against the tight hole of her anus. In a flash, Ali's intentions became frighteningly clear and Leigh let out a horrified wail.

"No! Ali, please don't." She tried to pull away, but Jurgen's hands held her firm as his magnificent cock continued its thrusting. "I don't like it Ali."

"Quiet!" Even as Ali continued plunging her greedy sex onto the dildo while agitating her own thrumming clitoris, she pushed against the puckered skin of her friend's secret entrance.

"Ali!"

It was more of a scream than a word as Leigh felt the finger force its way inside. Fire ripped through her as the way was breached and the long fingernail and finger disappeared inside, bringing a blood curdling shriek to her lips and a chilling smile to Ali's.

Thrilling need drove Ali onward, greedily seeking her own orgasm. As she continued to thrust downward, she drove her finger in and out mercilessly, listening to her friend's sobs as her curvaceous body shuddered under the dual onslaught from penis and finger.

The floodgates burst and tears gushed from Leigh's pale eyes as her mind emptied itself of everything but the registration of pain. She couldn't stand the agony as the inferno spread, lighting up her insides as she was violated both front and back with nothing but a membrane separating cock from finger. She screamed, a terrible sound that filled the room with piercing noise.

Seconds later, Leigh was still screaming, but the tone had changed. It was as if something shattered inside her as her muscles went into spasm; her climax ripped through her with unequalled ferocity. In the same moment, Jurgen gave one final thrust and filled her sex with jet after jet of thick, hot liquid, knowing that Ali would make him suffer terribly for it over the next few days.

Ali threw back her head. The veins in her neck stood out tautly as she let out a shriek of her own as the convulsions shook her. Shaking her head in wild abandon, she listened to the sobbing Leigh with her insides joyously ablaze. Still impaled on the dildo, she speared John with a cold glance and relished his humiliation and unrequited lust that had him shaking wretchedly.

She laughed a cold-blooded laugh - life was wonderful.

CHAPTER ELEVEN

Things were beginning to get Leigh down. It was clear by now that the absent receptionist wasn't ever coming back, which dramatically increased her workload. The ideal situation would have been to have at least four receptionists, two to cover morning surgery with another two to cover evenings. However, Owen insisted that the budget wouldn't stretch to that, and still hadn't even taken on a replacement for the girl who had left, though Terence had hinted that a new receptionist could be joining the practice soon.

As Spring turned to Summer, Leigh grew more lonely and confused; her very posture had a despondency about it. Until Ali's return a few weeks ago, Leigh's life had been great, but suddenly everything was falling apart.

Owen's increasingly sour moods led to more threats; his constant sexual demands and late night visits to her house had her nearing breaking point. Not since her mother had taken off to open a bar in Spain had she felt so alone.

Even Terence seemed distant and had stopped responding to her teasing. And a couple of days after his return from Blackpool, after Errol had seen one particular flu patient at the surgery, he'd dumped her without so much as a word of explanation. On reflection, the reason wasn't too hard to fathom, since that patient had been John Micklem. He and Errol had always been friendly, since Errol was a frequent visitor to the Town Crier. It was her guess that that bastard Micklem had let something slip about Leigh's involvement in his degradation. And Errol, fearing for his own reputation, had obviously decided that it would be better not to associate with her.

Worse still was that Ali never seemed to be in to her calls, even Jurgen failed to pick up the phone. It had been three weeks since her visit to Ali's apartment, and she'd left numerous messages on her answerphone which were never returned.

Things really hit rock bottom one Friday evening, when having forgotten to put away the patients' notes after surgery she popped along to Owen's consulting room, with the intention of trying to win back some of the self esteem that was fading fast. Perhaps if she turned on the little-girl voice and innocent adolescent look, she could turn the tables on Owen once and for all.

Besides, it might be fun to try and by God, she could do with some of that right now.

The door was ajar. She didn't bother to knock but walked straight in, and was brought up sharply by the scene that confronted her. Owen was standing by the couch with one of his patients, a girl of eighteen. Perversely, the first thought that entered her mind was one of jealousy - she'd been replaced by a younger model.

"Put your hand there," he said, oblivious to Leigh's presence in the doorway as he placed the girl's hand over the bulge in his trousers. "I know you think of me as your kindly old doctor, perhaps even a grandfather."

"Not at all", the girl answered politely, clearly uncomfortable with the situation but not sure what to do to escape from it.

Leigh felt sick as she heard the old cliché.

"You're the only one I can turn to. My wife doesn't understand me."

Momentarily frozen to the spot, Leigh's conscience told her she should get help. The man had to be stopped! But if Owen ever found out it was Leigh who raised the alarm, her life wouldn't be worth living.

Transfixed, she watched as the girl extracted his cock.

Cold fingers of panic gripped her throat. Trembling, she covered her mouth with her hands. She simply had to get help! He had to be stopped! But not only that - she had to pay him back. No one had the right to use her as if she was some backstreet whore and then throw her aside like last year's desk diary.

And then a thought struck her - Ali would know what to do.

Without thinking it through, she spun round and made a dash from the room, knocking over chairs and scattering magazines from the tables as she tore through the waiting room and out into the fresh air.

**

Twenty minutes later, the phone rang in Ali's bedroom, where she was happily engaged in administering discipline to a most delightful, heart-shaped backside.

She snatched up the receiver with an impatient, "yes?"

"Sorry to bother you, Mistress," the security guard's breathing was heavy and ragged, "but that pretty redhead's on her way up."

"Thanks, George."

Ali's heart leaped as she replaced the receiver, and the quivers that had peppered her insides with arousal while thrashing the girl now transformed themselves into full-blooded throbs and shudders. At last her tactics of inattention and feigned apathy had paid off; she'd known Leigh would come running to her sooner or later.

Smiling, Ali returned to the foot of the bed. Placing her hands on the young girl's buttocks, she scraped her long fingernails over the scarlet weals that criss-crossed the tender flesh, smiling grimly as the girl flinched. Throwing the crop aside, she addressed her tersely as she set about releasing her ankles and wrists from the black metal uprights that formed the structure of the modern, top-of-the-range four poster.

"You've come a long way since your first visit, Cindy, and can take thirty lashes without so much as a whimper. I'm very impressed - so impressed that I've decided to give you another twenty. But for the moment you've been reprieved, we'll carry on with this later. I've got an unexpected visitor on the way up, so you've got a chance to impress me with your waitressing skills, which were piss-poor on your last visit! Any cock-ups tonight will be dealt with most severely. I want you to open the door to my guest and show her through to the lounge, where you'll serve us drinks."

Cindy gave a little bob.

"Yes, Mistress Blackheart."

Ali looked the girl over and congratulated herself on the way the heavily boned blue Basque improved the girl's figure. True, it was rather restrictive and seemed to affect her breathing, but Ali felt it was worth it. The small but nevertheless exquisite breasts were pushed together and raised tantalizingly by the half cups, and the tightness of the waist gave quite a nice swell to her hips. The back view was much improved also and as she headed for the door Ali noticed how the striped, heart-shaped bottom appeared fleshier and swayed nicely above the thighs, beautifully emphasised by the lacy stocking tops.

Cindy had also learnt to walk elegantly without tottering over in the high stilettos and held her head high as if she were proud of her enslaved condition. The leather collar which Cindy's true master now required her to wear, at Ali's suggestion, was most flattering as were the wrist restraints, and Ali made a mental note to equip Leigh similarly as soon as possible.

The door was opened at Leigh's third ring. She blinked a couple of times in disbelief and her mouth dropped open with surprise at the sight of the young, blue-Basqued girl. Misery clutched at her heart. No wonder Ali hadn't bothered to answer her calls; she'd clearly replaced her with a new friend, a girl that was little older than the patient she'd seen with Owen!

"I...I'm s... sorry..." she could have kicked herself for stammering like an idiot, but it was difficult to talk while choking back tears, "I... I'll come back... later."

"Mistress will see you now." The girl held the door open. "Please, follow me."

Feeling awkward, Leigh dabbed at her nose with a tissue as she followed the girl into the lounge, her scandalized gaze fixed to the marks on Cindy's bottom. Fear clutched at her stomach muscles but so did something else, something she still couldn't come to terms with as the memory of Ali's riding crop cutting into her own flesh came flooding back.

By now she should have been used to Ali's surprises, but nothing could have prepared her for the sight that greeted her and made her give a startled, "Ooooo!"

Naked as always, Jurgen was on the floor in the centre of the room. His chin was touching the polished floorboards and he was resting on his elbows with his backside facing the kitchen doorway and stuck in the air. Ali sat on his back like a pixie, cross-legged and smoking a cigar.

His ankles were held open by the spreader bar and his hands were cuffed behind his head. Even from where she stood Leigh could see his huge erection.

"Bloody hell, Ali! What's going on?"

"Leigh! What a lovely surprise."

Ali took a drag from the cigar, turned her face towards Jurgen's head, then blew out the smoke. She smiled with satisfaction as he coughed.

"Please," Ali indicated the leather-topped footstool beside the kitchen door, "pull up a seat. The girl will only be a tick with our drinks." She took another drag.

Ali's commanding tone precluded argument. Leigh went to fetch the stool and on the way back was presented with the sight of Jurgen's backside and thick thighs, startlingly bruised and covered by a network of deep ridges. His huge balls, dangling between his legs like a dog's, were imprisoned by a thick metal ring which had a chain fixed to it, the other end of which was secured to a hook above the kitchen door. And that wasn't all. As Leigh placed the stool on the floor and sat facing Ali, she noticed there was a second chain attached to the front of the ring and pulled taut in the other direction, where it was secured to a similar hook on the opposite wall.

"Comfortable, Leigh?" Ali asked affably, as if the whole bizarre situation were the most natural thing in the world.

In fact, Leigh was crushingly embarrassed and felt at a distinct disadvantage having to look up at her imperious friend, but decided it was probably better not to mention it. Instead, her attention was drawn to Cindy who approached carrying a silver tray on which were two glasses of champagne. As she took a sip, Leigh gave Ali's outfit the once-over.

As usual, she wore high heeled leather boots coming up to her mid calf, even Leigh had to admit they set off her legs nicely. Her black hold-ups left a gap of flesh between the lacy tops and the hem of the short, black leather skirt which was split at one side from hem to waistband.

With it she wore a wide, black leather belt that cinched her small waist and her sleeveless, low-cut, black top hugged her figure beautifully, leaving nothing to the imagination as her nipples struggled to poke their way through the soft leather. Once again, she wore gloves that reached almost to her armpits.

Ali took her glass from the tray, giving Cindy instructions to stand in the corner until she was needed. Turning her attention to Leigh, she said,

"you look bloody miserable, as always. Look Babe, I've known since I got back from Europe that something's bothering you. So are you going to sit there ogling this wimp's tackle all night...," she gave Jurgen's thigh a vicious kick, "or open your mouth?"

Leigh coloured up at being caught staring and immediately averted her eyes. While Cindy kept their glasses topped up, Leigh blurted out the whole sordid story, how it had all started with Owen and how he'd threatened her. She brought Ali right up to date with the latest development, but for some reason left out the bit about feeling neglected.

Without looking at him, Ali flicked ash between Jurgen's buttocks, then reached down and gave the chain a tug, making him yell. She returned her knowing gaze to Leigh.

"Don't tell me, you thought it would be a good idea if someone, that someone being me, put the good doctor in his place once and for all. Right?"

"Well, yes... I thought perhaps you could do to him what you did to John. After all, Owen deserves it..." she flicked her eyes to Jurgen then back to Ali's hard features, "and John didn't."

"Is that what you think? Even if I tell you that a couple of years ago he had a fling with your mother?"

Leigh shrugged. "It seems she had flings all over town before she went off to Spain to open her bar."

Ali smiled enigmatically as she considered whether or not to tell.

"I guess bars do have something to do with it..." She snapped her fingers. "Girl! Brandy!"

Leigh declined the offer of a brandy and put her hand over her glass when Cindy attempted to refill it with champagne. But Ali would brook no argument and insisted she had just one more. Reluctantly, Leigh relented and sipped half-heartedly.

"They all bloody deserve it, Babe, every chicken-hearted one of them!"

Sipping her brandy and watching Leigh thoughtfully, Ali struggled to batten down the lust that bubbled away inside her. Her smile was thin as, to Leigh's horror, she stubbed her cigar out on Jurgen's backside. When he made no sound of protest, Leigh thought better of making one herself, but listened as Ali continued icily.

"If I do this for you - if you really want to go through with it, I'll want something in return."

"Yes, anything."

"Anything? You're sure of that?"

Leigh raked her fingers through her hair in a gesture of defiance as she flashed Ali an impatient look, "I've said so, haven't I?"

"Ok, keep your hair on! Just as long as you understand. I'll pop by the surgery on Monday to see him."

She winked, then gave Leigh that look she remembered from years ago, the one against which she had no defence - the one that always won her over and invariably resulted in her getting in trouble.

"But look - for it to really work, Leigh, you'll have to watch the proceedings." Horrified, Leigh was about to protest, but Ali raised a hand to check her. "I think it'd probably be best if you moved in here, for a short while at least. That way he won't be able to get at you without my knowing, and it'll mean you'll always be on hand in case I need you. Don't worry, I'll make sure he doesn't take it out on you afterwards. Are you working in the morning?"

"Yes. There's always an emergency surgery on Saturdays."

"Ok. Come back here afterwards. While you're out, I'll get someone round to your place to move some of your things in here."

"What about...?" Leigh nodded towards Cindy, who stood quietly in the corner with her back straight, feet slightly apart and her hands behind her back, then at Jurgen.

"She'll be gone by the time you get here. And you'll be quite safe with this piece of low life." Ali cast a glance at Jurgen, then studied Leigh's disconcerted expression as she elaborated. "He wouldn't dare touch you without my say-so! To go against me," she warned, "is to invite punishment."

Slipping off Jurgen's back, Ali stepped over him and instructed Cindy to fetch her another cigar, already lighted, while she herself collected a many-thonged whip from the rack in her bedroom.

Paying no heed to poor Cindy who spluttered terribly as she drew on the cigar to light it, Ali stalked back across the room and stood alongside Jurgen. Cindy scurried towards her with the tip of the cigar glowing and Ali snatched it from her, instructing tersely that she return to her corner. Then, after taking several drags, under Leigh's outraged gaze Ali stuffed the unlit end up Jurgen's back passage.

Straightening up again, she adjusted her position and stood with her legs slightly apart to brace herself. With her face set in a terrifying scowl of concentration, Ali pulled back her arm and took aim. Then, with deadly accuracy, she cracked the whip sadistically across his scrotum.

Jurgen let out a fierce cry and the force of the stroke made him jerk against his bonds, making the chains jangle alarmingly as they tugged his balls.

Again Ali struck, this time curling the cruel thongs and catching him round his thigh and across his penis, before thrashing him in earnest. Bringing the lash down across his thighs and then his back, taking care each time to avoid the cigar, she aimed each stroke so that the leather strands curled themselves around either the front of his thighs or underneath to catch his belly.

When his body glistened with a sheen of sweat, Ali wrapped the thongs around the handle and placed the whip between his teeth. Triumphantly, she took up her crossed-legged position sitting on his back, making him wince as her weight made contact with his savagely flayed skin.

Without a hint of remorse she smiled across at the gaping Leigh. She ran the tip of her tongue over her red-glossed lips as a flurry of anticipation warmed her loins. This was all so easy; she couldn't have planned it better herself.

"You'd better stay here tonight. The guest room isn't ready, so you'd better share mine." Ali swigged back the remainder of her brandy. "Remember how we always said what fun it'd be to share?"

Leigh's brittle nerves jangled alarmingly; she was afraid. Not just of Ali's depravity but of her own inexperience. Until now, she'd never slept with a woman and wasn't sure what was required of her. Where did one put one's hands? And what about the other end- should one touch it or not? Or were you just supposed to turn over and go to sleep? She didn't want to look stupid, nor reveal any of the repulsion and shame that mingled with her curiosity.

Leigh sighed dreamily as Ali's warm skin brushed against her own as they lay side by side in Ali's four-poster, and sudden, erotic whorls in her belly caught her unawares. Ali's very nakedness sent ripples of emotions pulsing through her that she didn't know how to deal with. The uncomfortable mixture of guilt and shame side by side with satiny bliss intensified as she yielded to Ali's subversive charisma.

Ali pulled her closer, her strong arms enfolding her in a warm, comforting embrace which erased all memories of cruelty from her mind. Resting her head against Ali's breasts, Leigh listened contentedly to the beating of Ali's heart, and realized that her own was pounding with equal vigour.

Consumed by the conflicting emotions, excitement took Leigh's breath away as Ali's gentle touch on her cheek smoothed the soft strands of hair from her face. She made no objection when Ali's fingers skimmed down her neck, slowly and sensually, until they closed around Leigh's hardening nipple. Softly and skilfully, without a trace of the sadism that had gone before, Ali coaxed it into a peak.

Unable to contain the murmurs of delight that welled up inside her trembling body, Leigh made little mewing sounds. Ali's response was to manoeuvre herself into a position whereby she was able to bring her head down, clamping her hungry lips over Leigh's to silence her with kisses.

More aware than ever before of her own femininity, if Leigh had any remaining shreds of doubt, they dissolved in a mist of warm sensation as their tongues entwined in an erotic voyage of discovery. Never had she experienced such a rush of euphoria and her heart took up an erratic thudding that matched the pounding in her clitoris as it escaped from its protective hood.

Forsaking Leigh's nipple, Ali eased herself onto her elbows and levered herself upward. As Ali settled her full weight upon her friend's curvaceous body, already glistening with beads of moisture, Leigh arched her back in an effort to grind her mons against Ali's. There was a furnace between Leigh's legs and her dampening quim cried out for relief.

She felt Ali's breath hot against her face, breath that fractured excitedly as Ali slipped her hands beneath Leigh's bottom and caressed her buttocks, swirling her fingers over the satin flesh, squeezing gently.

And, feeling strangely detached from reality, Leigh revelled in the glory of Ali's arousal, knowing that it was she, Leigh, who was responsible. She'd always loved to turn men on, but had never dreamt that she could generate such intense emotions in another woman. Armed with her new knowledge, she wallowed in the inner glow and strange, new sense of herself.

She crooked her leg across Ali's back and, after a moment of high voltage kissing, rolled her sideways. Now, as they lay face to face, Leigh's own arousal eclipsed anything that had gone before as her nimble fingers slid downward on an exploratory journey, until she found the hard bud at the apex of Ali's labia.

Tentatively, she pressed her finger against it, stroking it with small, circular movements that soon had Ali groaning.

Ali's eager fingers began a reciprocal caress and, before long, the two young women were bucking and writhing together, each lost in a world of joyful warmth as they moved ever closer to a devastating climax. And when it came, they reached it together, shuddering and screaming as one as their heads snapped backward and their muscles tensed.

Afterward, as she lay exhausted in Ali's arms, the embers of afterglow nuzzled every fibre of Leigh's being. With a smile hovering around her lips, she acknowledged this as the turning point in her life.

CHAPTER TWELVE

A li almost whooped with joy as she opened the front door to Leigh after receiving the call from Security. After everything that had happened, how could Leigh still be so unsuspecting?

"I'm done in!" Leigh's lavish breasts heaved as she struggled to speak and catch her breath at the same time. "It's been really busy at the surgery this morning."

Ali's thin lips merely twitched upwards as she relieved Leigh of her handbag. Mulling it over, she realized that Leigh's self image was quite different from the actuality; Leigh fooled herself that she was worldly-wise when, as far as Ali was concerned, the reality was far more peachy. It was that often timid, childlike quality about Leigh that had always set a storm brewing in Ali's loins and got her juices flowing.

When they'd first met, Leigh had been overly cautious, the sort of girl who wouldn't have dared do anything if it hadn't been for Ali's particular brand of encouragement. In time, Ali had been able to persuade her to do almost anything, invariably leaving Leigh in the lurch while she escaped scot-free. To her credit, Leigh's loyalty had been unstinting and she'd never once dropped Ali in it. Yet never in her wildest fantasies had Ali imagined that Leigh could have retained so much of her trusting innocence, an innocence which would make Leigh's slide into decadence all the more exquisite.

Mentally, Ali gave herself a slap on the back. At first she'd been afraid of scaring Leigh off but in the event the implementation of her plans had been almost too easy. There was a thrumming in her breasts as she imagined the hours of pleasure that lay ahead.

"Is the kettle on?" Leigh kicked off her shoes in the hallway. "I'm dying for a cuppa!"

"Go through to the lounge. I'll have Jurgen bring you some tea in a minute."

"Thanks, but I don't mind making it myself."

"That's what he's here for! Besides, he's preparing lunch and hates to be disturbed while he's working," Ali pointed out

Suddenly ill at ease, Leigh shrugged. "Ok! Look, I don't want to be a nuisance. If you just show me my room,"

"I'll give you a tour of the place later."

"Well, at least point me in the right direction. I want to get my things sorted; I need to check that you've had the right things brought over."

"Everything you'll need is there." Ali placed a firm hand on Leigh's forearm. "I said I'd show you later. In the meantime, go through to the lounge and take it easy. I've got a few calls to make, then I have to take a shower. I shouldn't be long."

Ali's frosty smile should have warned of the treachery to come. Instead, Leigh's insides melted as, with a swift movement that took her by surprise, Ali's strong arms tightened around her and drew her closer.

Overcome with languorous wanting, Leigh was dangerously unaware that the warm embrace had switched in a trice from one of exquisite tenderness to one of restraint.

Ali pressed her malevolent, glossed lips against Leigh's and planted a fraudulent kiss of such sweetness that Leigh dissolved into the moment as tingles spiralled through her. She gave herself up willingly, joyful in the knowledge that Ali would always be there for her.

Ali released her hold and propelled Leigh forwards.

"Take your clothes off and I'll join you later. Think of me as a flying instructor - I'll take you to heights you thought it was impossible to reach."

Impressed with the analogy, Leigh giggled helplessly.

"Is that a promise?" she chirped in her tinkling, girlie tones.

"Fucking count on it!"

With that, Ali left the room.

Floating on air, Leigh combed her fingers through the abundance of her shining hair as she went through to the lounge and followed Ali's suggestion. She shrugged out of her clothes, folding them carefully and laying them across the back of the sofa.

In the background she could hear Jurgen moving around in the kitchen; cupboards opening and closing, the chinking of crockery and clatter of cutlery gave the place an air of domesticity. Leigh smiled at the normality of it all.

She left her hold-ups on; she always felt sexy when she stood in nothing but her stockings. She slewed her glance downward and wasn't at all surprised that her cherry nipples were as hard as a couple of ball bearings. She skimmed her fingers lightly over her belly until they reached her red-fleeced mons and entwined her fingers with the coarse curls.

Tendrils of arousal flipped the mischief switch to stand-by. Here she was, almost naked and burning up with lust, while in the kitchen there was a gorgeous hunk of a man with an elephantine dick.

Well, waste not, want not.

Ali hadn't said what time she wanted lunch, but Jurgen had finished with the preparation and was ready to serve whenever she commanded. There were always zillions of things to be done about the place, and he set about his other chores with his usual enthusiasm. Ali was a hard taskmaster, and to skimp on any task was to risk her wrath.

She'd want to spend a few minutes with her new toy before taking a shower, as well as ringing Cindy's master with a progress report. The youngster had been in tears when the chauffeur had collected her. For no apparent reason, Ali had denied Cindy food since the previous afternoon and, despite her improved waitressing and obedience, had given her a savage flogging first thing that morning that had left her so weak she could hardly stand.

Naked as always, Jurgen was wiping over the cooker, an excessively large monstrosity in chrome which took up the greater part of the kitchen, when the door opened.

"Hello, Jurgen."

He turned towards the sound, to see Leigh standing in the doorway like the temptress from hell, her red-gold mane of tangled curls falling about her shoulders. Gloriously naked apart from black, lacy-topped hold-ups that contrasted perfectly with her pale skin, her exuberant breasts heaved alluringly with every breath. His eyes alighted on the mass of red hair that adorned her mons and his cock stirred eagerly.

"I was just wondering," she said tilting her head to one side and giving him a coquettish look from beneath her fine lashes, "if I could make a cup of tea?"

He'd been given strict orders not to fraternise; he was nothing but a worthless slave with no rights to normal conversation. Still, they were alone- who'd know?

"I'll do it. Sit down." He beckoned her in and glanced nervously towards the door. "Where's the mistress?"

The mischief switch flickered, then lit up the red light as it switched itself on. "Oh, she won't be ready for lunch for ages." Emphasising the last word, she gave him her most seductive smile. She slipped her finger in her mouth and made sucking noises.

He pointed to the chrome stool in the corner, watched entranced as her succulent buttocks made contact with the black leather seat, and gave her the benefit of the doubt. Obviously she didn't understand the situation here, that what she was doing to him bordered on torture.

Struggling vainly to ignore the rising heat in his balls, he pulled down the table top that fitted flush against the wall.

"Not very big, is it?" she trilled, staring at his penis, magnificent even in repose. Realizing at once that the accidental implication made her sound like Ali, she employed all her skills to make light of the situation.

"Sorry, I didn't mean that!" she giggled and looked away quickly, as if embarrassed. She slipped her finger in and out of her mouth a couple of times. Sweeping her gaze over the room, she tried out her girlie voice on him. "I meant the kitchen - the kitchen's not very big in comparison to the rest of the place."

Momentarily taken in by her finely tuned come-on, he let his guard slip and foolishly allowed himself to be drawn into conversation.

"A casualty of Mistress Blackheart's rebuilding scheme. She had the kitchen cut down to half its original size to make an extra room." He gave a snort of derision that was worthy of Ali herself. "If you can call a small, windowless cubicle a room. It's dark and airless. I should know - it's my room."

Refusing to be taken in by his attempt to cause bad blood between herself and Ali, she scoffed at the very idea.

"Don't be ridiculous. She's not that mean."

"How little you know her! The woman's a hard-faced witch. I swear it's no bigger than a cupboard. And there's another just like it down the hall. They don't even have wardrobes."

There was only one way to stop his lies. She flicked her tongue up and down the length of one finger and opened her thighs, slipping her other hand between her legs. Her pinkening labia glistened tantalizingly. Using two fingers, she held open the outer lips to display the juicy, red inner lips before slipping her forefinger inside the inviting channel.

"So where do you keep your clothes?"

"I don't need any. The Mistress doesn't permit me to leave the apartment."

"So it's true then," her eyes skidded down his magnificent torso and came to rest on his cock which stood out at a 90 degree angle, "you're starkers all the time?"

"The Mistress gave my clothes to some girl who has a stall at a car boot sale to raise money for homeless cats." Usually so guarded, in the grip of Leigh's flirtatious charms his tongue ran away with him. "The only things in the room are a hard mattress, one pillow and one sheet - and metal rings sunk into the floorboards at each corner so she can chain me up at night if the fancy takes her."

She plucked her finger from her mouth as her voice rose a couple of octaves.

"Oh come on! You don't expect me to believe that!" She was having too much fun to be sidetracked by his lies. Seeing the effect she was having on him, she began to rub her slippery pussy with more fervour, and ran the tip of her tongue over her lips slowly before asking flippantly, "why would she chain you up?"

"It's her right - I'm her slave."

Stunned, her finger stopped its rubbing. "Slave? Now you're being bloody stupid!"

Nevertheless, there was something about his voice that unsettled her. As she tried to make sense of his words, she had no way of knowing that her innocent expression that sent bolts of lightning straight to his cock would land her in so much trouble.

"Believe what you want- you'll find out soon enough."

There was an uncomfortable feeling uncurling in the pit of her stomach as the pieces came together, the way coloured fragments of glass in a kaleidoscope form a pattern.

"No, I won't believe it," she said without conviction. The way Ali spoke to him, the way she humiliated him... it must mean something. "Surely a man like you..."

"A man like me? You don't know the first thing about me."

Resentment raised its ugly head as the bitter humiliation of the dominated creature that he'd become took up the familiar battle against the electrifying thrill that same humiliation always provoked. As his inner battle raged so his lust increased.

Shame won; Jurgen lowered his eyes submissively and admitted "Yes, I'm a slave, to the most lascivious, savage, hard-hearted woman alive."

Even now, she was eager to defend her friend against his absurd allegations, though her fiery denial of what was obviously the truth didn't ring true even to her own ears.

"You're way out of line, Buster! I know she's tough, but she's not as bad as you make out. I, more than anyone, know she's done some wild things in the past," she shook her head furiously from side to side, "but she's my best friend and I won't believe it! I've known her for years!"

"You wouldn't call her 'friend' if you knew what she's got planned for you!"

Leigh's bottom lip quivered. "W...what do you mean?"

"What I say."

He swept his eyes over the sensuous curves of her perfectly formed body. She was trembling. Frightened, she'd no idea how much more appealing that made her. He came and stood beside her and reached out his hand. He smoothed her luxuriant hair, at the same time slipping his free hand down to cup her breast. There was no need to tweak her nipple to tumescence- it was already twice its normal size. If he didn't fuck the little darling soon, he'd get real cranky!

Her breasts were ripe, heavy and flushed a delicate shade of pink. In spite of her flare-up, she didn't push him away. On the contrary, she smiled invitingly. It was plain to see why the mistress ached to dominate her- anyone would. And for one moment, he was back in his homeland among his own slave girls.

Placing her hand over his, she allowed him to slide his downward. His cock twitched as his hand skimmed over her satin skin, over her belly and down between her thighs. She let her own hand slip away as he eased her thighs apart and used his eager finger to trace the line of her slit. She was so trusting and sweet, he really should warn her of the dangers that lay ahead. But he'd always been partial to watching the weals rise on a pretty girl, however much he tried to convince himself otherwise.

"The person you knew as Ali no longer exists. But Mistress Blackheart is alive and kicking," he gave a little laugh, "usually me in the ribs! She's rich, powerful, and..."

"I know these apartments were aimed at the more affluent, discerning buyer..." she paused to consider, "but how on earth did Ali?"

"The Mistress has resources." Working his finger enthusiastically in her deliciously warm, wet pussy, he advised, "just do as she says and everything will be fine. Otherwise, you'll end up in the playroom."

As the tension drained away, she threw back her head and laughed sneeringly, "scary!" tossing her mane of red-gold curls. "You mean she's got a snooker table or something? She always was pretty handy with a cue."

"You stupid bitch! If you won't listen then you deserve everything you get." His tone changed and his words were suddenly urgent. "We've just got time for a quick fuck."

Again she laughed.

"Oh come on! A man that won't bloody sneeze without permission is hardly going to risk a fuck!"

It was as if an explosion went off in his head. Galvanised into action, he snatched his finger from her vagina so roughly that it made her cry out. He seized her wrist and yanked her to her feet. She stumbled awkwardly as he pitched her forward, to sprawl inelegantly against the cooker. In a flash he was behind her and corrected her position so that her belly pressed against the cold metal and her upper body was leaning across the cooled hotplates. As she gripped the sides of the cooker, his cock speared upward. He pressed her head downwards.

Instinct alone opened her legs. He guided his penis, long and hot, towards her juicing pussy lips which peeled back obligingly.

An electric charge passed between slave and seductress as his hungry phallus forced its way inside. Relishing the tightness of her delightful hole, he buried his shaft up to the hilt while his hands closed around her generously proportioned breasts. Savagely pistoning in and out like a man deprived of sex for too long, he worked himself into a frenzy, making her squeal as he shoved her hard against the metal.

"If the mistress gets an inkling of this," he felt her shudder beneath him as his words came out on ragged breaths, "we're both dead!"

***

As she lay contentedly on her back on the lounge floor, still naked except for her black hold-ups, the afternoon sun streamed in through the slits in the blinds and threw horizontal stripes across Leigh's body. Lazily, she slid her foot across the wooden floor to raise her knee, inadvertently flashing her glistening crop of red pubic hair and fleshy labia.

The illicit sex with Jurgen had been the most wonderful she'd ever experienced. Her orgasm had been demolishing in its intensity, he'd had to stuff a piece of kitchen towel in her mouth to stop her screaming when she'd climaxed.

Sun-warmed and bathing in the soft caress that was the afterglow of wonderful sex, her face broke into a smile. Blissfully unaware of the silvery trails that adorned her thighs as she crossed her right leg over the left, she rested her ankle against her lower thigh and drifted into a peaceful sleep.

The first she knew of Ali's presence was the tip of something hard pressing against her lips. She flung her eyes open to see Ali, treacherous as ice and twice as nasty, standing with one booted foot beside her head while the other rested on her face, the wicked spiked heel forcing Leigh's lips apart.

CHAPTER THIRTEEN

"Fucking with the house boy's worn you out has it, my little slut?"

Ali's frosty gaze froze Leigh's blood as she swivelled the ridiculously high heel back and forth between Leigh's soft, pink lips, squashing her face beneath the sole of her boot.

"Don't tell me, you thought I didn't know?" Pausing only to laugh at her friend's anguish, Ali's eyes shone with undiluted cruelty. "I know everything that goes on here. You'll be punished, of course. And Jurgen? I've already dealt with him."

Dumbstruck, Leigh made to move her arms to shove Ali off, but to her horror discovered they were tied at the wrists with thick cord that was already cutting into her tender flesh.

Momentarily gripped by a frisson of alarm, it took a supreme effort of will to overcome the trembling that shook her body, knowing that one false move would mean disaster. Somehow, she'd slipped headlong into a nightmare. For the first time she realized how vulnerable she really was, and a croak of protest escaped her throat.

"Don't make excuses! I demand total discipline and unquestioning loyalty." The sheen of Ali's slicked-back hair matched the sheen in her black eyes. "I'm Mistress in this establishment, and everyone else is here to serve my commands. And guess what? You're right at the bottom of the pile. Don't expect any favours. I'll come down extra hard on you. This is your first lesson in submission - my boots are always cleaned by mouth, in this case, yours. Use your tongue and start with the heel, you can do the rest later."

Leigh shot Ali an accusatory gaze. She'd been in sticky situations many times before, courtesy of Ali and her wildness, with the result that tiny cracks had sometimes appeared in their relationship. In the end, Leigh had always been fearful of losing Ali's friendship and had been quick to paper over them. But this time it was more than a crack - it was a gaping chasm. As soon as she was able, she told herself resolutely, she must escape once and for all from Ali's clutches.

She had no choice but to admit the wicked spike into her soft, vulnerable mouth. It grazed her tongue as Ali applied gentle but nevertheless disconcerting pressure. As a melange of emotions tugged her this way and that, a dampness rose in her eyes and was mirrored between her legs.

Using the tip of her tongue to reach up as far as possible, Leigh licked at the spike.

With her skin tingling under Ali's mocking scrutiny, she slipped deeper and deeper into a black hole of despair. She flicked her eyes upward; Ali was standing over her like a demon encased in black leather.

The catsuit she wore moulded itself as perfectly to her body as the skin fits a grape. The only visible areas of flesh were her small hands with their long fingernails, her heavily made-up face and her red, engorged labia which protruded through a well-designed slit in the leather.

Leigh welcomed the sudden withdrawal of the spike with a sigh of relief, then pressed her lips firmly together when Ali stomped her foot on the floor alongside her head. However, her relief was short lived as with quicksilver speed, Ali pressed the spike of the other boot against her mouth.

"I've got two boots, Bitch!"

This time, Leigh's resolve was strong and she kept her lips tightly closed.

Ali's satin-toned voice was quiet yet commandingly chilling as her coal black stare burned into the redhead's pale flesh. Like damp tendrils of mist, malevolence filled the air.

"What's this? The brainless tart finally has a will of her own? Too late, Babe, too late! When I said I wanted something in return for helping you with your problem, you agreed. 'Anything' you said. That's the deal, Leigh. It's too late to back out now. You try going back on your word and I'll personally give your Owen any help he wants in destroying you."

The spike gained entry to Leigh's yielding mouth. She tried not to listen, but Ali's vehement words continued to rain down on her.

"You do exactly as I say, got it? If I tell you to stand naked in the street with a bucket over your head or empty your bladder in the middle of the shopping mall then that's what you'll do. Understand?"

Curling her tongue around the vicious spike made it impossible to speak, and Leigh only managed a tiny squawk of dissent, which brought an immediate response from Ali in the form of the sole pressing down harder against her face.

"You'd better understand!"

Leigh could smell the sweet musk of Ali's lust, just as she could see the droplets of honey that dripped from her elongated labial lips.

A chill shudder travelled along the invisible ribbon that linked Leigh's clitoris to her breasts as she caught sight of the evil looking whip which Ali tapped against her leg, the long, leather thongs curling harmlessly around her booted ankle.

With her throat arid with fear, Leigh's skin was burning up. Ali's words swam in her head as she wrestled desperately to contain the shudders that racked her body as she imagined the terrible spike disappearing down her throat. Keeping her eyes and mouth wide open and one long leg still crossed over the other, Leigh began to lick the offending spike, pausing only a moment in her task when Ali swivelled round to face her feet.

Again, Leigh sighed as the dangerous spike was withdrawn. She closed her eyes tightly. A sob, half relief and half despair escaped from her lips as Ali took a couple of steps backward so that she was standing behind Leigh's head.

Leigh should have known it was coming; after all, she heard the Swish! but it wasn't until the horrendous eruption of fire which accompanied the Crack! across her belly that she realized what had happened. Her eyes flew open at the same moment as her shrill scream shattered a crystal brandy glass, for which she immediately received another lash. A reflex reaction made Leigh's long legs shoot out straight as her entire body bounced under the force that drove the breath from her.

But before she'd had time to sit up, a further line of fire was drawn across the soft skin of her belly. She flung out her tethered wrists and spread her hands across her belly in a desperate bid shield herself.

Getting into her stride, Ali was having none of it and brought the whip down across Leigh's hands. Again and again the whip came down. Once it just missed her breasts as the wicked fronds curled around her torso. Leigh yowled at the top of her voice, then sobbed so violently it shook her shoulders.

"Ali! Stop!"

"Stop? I've hardly got started!"

Lights exploded at the back of Leigh's brain as another lash caught her belly. Again she screamed.

"Please stop! you're hurting me!"

"And you've no idea how long I've waited."

Ali raised the whip threateningly. Spitefully, she waited a few moments to study the cold light of fear in her friend's eyes, drinking in the erotic image of Leigh's sensual, trembling body as it lay coated with an attractive sheen of sweat. Then she brought the lash crashing down again.

Leigh's head thrashed from side to side, her voluminous hair dripping with sweat and plastered to her face.

Ali paused again, enjoying the miscellany of emotions that crossed Leigh's face. With sadistic delight she waited until Leigh, thinking it was over, flicked open her eyes, before bringing the whip down again. Aiming low, Ali cut the skin close to Leigh's red bush, taking care not to catch her sex; she'd save that pleasure for another day.

Scarlet weals already criss-crossed the soft, white flesh of Leigh's belly. Even so, Ali hadn't done yet. Correcting her stance, she brought the whip down ferociously across the tops of Leigh's thighs, where the soft flesh contrasted so prettily with her stocking tops. Taking care to curl the fronds as she thrashed her friend in earnest, Ali feasted her gaze on the delightfully writhing girl who screamed fit to burst her lungs under the savage onslaught.

Leigh's treacherous nipples throbbed painfully, sending messages of arousal to her ever dampening quim, then bounced all the way back again. Bolts of lightning ricocheted through her as again the whip crashed down.

Slowly, she became aware that something had changed. She wasn't only screaming with pain; there was another feeling, too, something she didn't want to acknowledge as delicious. Quiveringly, she opened her mouth to let out a breathless groan as her excitement grew; the contradictory sensations of pleasure and pain were becoming blurred.

"That's better," Ali dropped the whip and walked round to stand by Leigh's feet, looking up the length of the soaked body before her, "now you're beginning to understand." She hunkered down and seized Leigh's ankles, imprisoning them in a grip as tight as any man's.

Leigh's skin diffused with colour. She was angry, not just with Ali but also with herself for allowing herself be beaten into submission. And she felt so unbearably humiliated. Pain wracked her body, set her skin on fire, and bombarded her senses with amazing new sensations that must surely be wrong.

As sanity edged its way back into her brain, Leigh made up her mind that she was going to survive this. With Ali still gripping her ankles and her wrists tied, she struggled into a sitting position.

"Ok, Ali, you've had your fun." Her hands dropped protectively between her legs. "When I asked for your help I didn't think it would be like this."

"What the fuck did you think it would be like? You're not stupid, you've seen what goes on here and you're right, it is fun! I get such a terrific buzz when I'm in control. I enjoy the sex, of course, but it's only part of it. It's the thrill of domination, the power that really turns me on. I get off on other people's pain and humiliation; and I've waited a long time to humiliate you!"

"You're mad!" Leigh moved her head decisively. She'd be better off handling Owen alone than staying here where things could only get worse; better the devil she knew than the one she thought she knew.

"I want to call our deal off. I'll start looking around for another job. There's a new receptionist starting on Monday, so Owen won't be able to bother me at work."

A sudden jerk on Leigh's legs made her topple backward and hit her head. Instead of concern, it was laughter that erupted from Ali's mouth as she began dragging Leigh across the floor. "But his wife will!"

"His wife? What the hell are you talking about?"

Ali mauled her with a hungry gaze that came to rest at the red apex of her thighs.

"Nina Brand; a nice woman. I met her in the Water Gardens. Afterwards, we went back to her place for a chat. She's got it into her head that her husband's having it off with his patients and, from what you've told me, she's right."

Glancing down at the quivering, sweating redhead, Ali gave in to temptation and told her how she'd seen Nina thrashing Terence Rankin's wife. The implication wasn't lost on Leigh who realized at once that if Nina also had a penchant for domination over women, then she, Leigh, was trapped whichever way she jumped.

The sinews of Ali's neck stood out tautly with the exertion of trying to talk while dragging Leigh bodily across the floor. But after only a moment's pause, she continued.

"What do you think she's going to do when she discovers he's fucking the receptionist too?"

Hauling her across the room once more, Ali opened the door and lugged her down the hall. On reaching another closed door, she released Leigh's ankles and let them fall to the floor.

"No, don't get up. Close your eyes."

Fearing now to do otherwise Leigh complied, only to find a second later that her eyes were held firmly closed by something tied across them and fastened behind her head. She heard an ominous creak as the door opened. Ali kicked her in the ribs to encourage her to get up, then grabbed her by the elbow and hauled her to her feet.

"Walk straight ahead."

Sightlessly, Leigh walked through the open doorway and into the room beyond.

"Stop!"

Leigh stopped.

"I thought it was time I showed you the playroom."

***

The pain was excruciating. Facing away from the wall bars, Leigh's chin rested on the floor, held in place by a metal frame that fitted across the back of her neck and was bolted to the floor on either side.

"You shouldn't have gone through to the kitchen when I told you not to," Ali informed her briskly. "Since you can't be trusted, you'll have to stay here awhile. This is only a taster of what happens if you disobey me."

With her shoulders touching the hard, white floorboards and her breasts flattened, her hands were cuffed behind her back.

Wide metal bands were fixed around her ankles chaining them to the wall bars. Her legs were raised several feet, thus lifting her abdomen clear of the floor, and dragged open so wide it felt as if she were being rent in two, causing her sex lips to gape.

However, Ali's sadistic nature still wasn't satisfied nor her lust sated, so she set about fixing metal cuffs around Leigh's elbows, and a chain to the cuffs at her wrists. Then, pulling Leigh's arms upward and back, she connected the end of the chain to the wall bars, at a point half way between Leigh's ankles.

"I told you Jurgen had already been dealt with," Ali told her as Leigh stared horror-stricken at the spectacle before her, wishing Ali had left her blindfold on.

Fear for her own skin had melted away, to be replaced by concern for Jurgen, whose torso bore deep lacerations from Ali's whip. Blindfolded and gagged, his head poked through an opening of a rigid, square board, made of some kind of black material. It was actually two pieces which slotted together, shaped to fit snugly around the neck. About an inch or so thick and two feet square, it rested on his shoulders.

His hands were drawn up on either side and kept in place by two special straps attached to the sides and fastened around his wrists. Positioned in the corner, he was standing on a low revolving platform, the size and shape of a dustbin lid. To stop him escaping, straps were fastened around his ankles and secured by chains to bolts in the turntable.

Lastly and most cruelly, his magnificent shaft had been pulled backwards through his legs. To hold it in position, Ali had fastened a tight leather strap around its girth, about half way along the shaft. This had a chain attached, which had been pulled tautly up his back, between his shoulder blades and fixed to the back of the wood on his shoulders by means of a hook.

Ali removed his blindfold so that, as he slowly revolved, he'd be tortured by the enchanting sight of Leigh.

Ali came and leaned against the wall bars, looking down the slope of Leigh's shackled body. "For fucking without permission you'll forfeit lunch, perhaps even dinner. If I have to starve you into submission, then so be it. And the same goes for him," she jerked her head towards the helplessly spinning Jurgen, "though it'll be much worse for him because he's got to cook it."

Crouching, Ali crept beneath Leigh's leg. She positioned herself crossed-legged between Leigh's open thighs and opened her own to expose the slit in her catsuit.

"What do you think, Jurgen? Was she worth it?"

Ali skimmed her fingers lightly over her own elongated pussy lips, before dipping one finger between them as she lowered her head.

Leigh couldn't contain the low-toned "Ooooo" as Ali's hot mouth descended over her wet, open quim. And, with her restricted movement, there was little she could do but give herself up to Ali's tongue as it snaked its way inside her tight channel.

Drowning in erotic euphoria, she didn't even try to hold at bay the delightful shudders and cramps that Ali's wicked tongue induced.

"You wanted to see your room," it was an hour or so later when Ali released her and shoved her through another door, "so here it is."

With her arms still cuffed at wrists and elbows, Leigh stood in the dim, windowless room and looked around bleakly. Just as Jurgen had claimed, there wasn't a stick of furniture, just a mattress with a pillow on the floor, covered with a plain white sheet. Nor had he lied about the metal rings - there was one at each corner, set into the floor. But there wasn't any sign of the belongings that she'd asked Ali to pick up for her, nor could she see any of her clothes.

As if reading her mind, Ali said, "I'll provide all your clothes and make-up. For the time being, you can carry on working, but I'll take you there and bring you back."

"It's ok," Leigh said sullenly, "you don't have to do that."

"Oh, but I do! You don't think I'm going to trust you out on your own?" Ali unfastened both sets of cuffs and, taking first one then the other of Leigh's arms in her hands, she began to rub the life back into them. "Lie down."

Life with Ali had always been chancy, a bit like walking barefoot on hot coals; if you believed you could survive you probably would. And Leigh had every intention of surviving this latest phase in their relationship, and so did as she was told without argument.

It was only when Ali stooped down and chained each ankle to the corresponding corner of the mattress that she began to get an inkling of the true nature of her predicament. And to bring the message home, Ali did the same with her wrists. Now, chained down in an X, Leigh had no choice but to listen as Ali ran through the rules that were to govern her life.

Ali stood upright and, with a devilish grin said caustically, "look at you- spread apart like the slut you are! If anyone needed to be kept in line, it's you. And I'm just the person to do it." She took a sadistic delight in observing how desolation and fear contorted Leigh's face, relishing the way disbelief turned to horror-stricken acceptance.

"The sooner you accept that you're totally subservient to me, the better it'll be for you. The demands of my body are the only ones that count around here. My word is law; you need my permission to scratch your bum, let alone fuck. Your wants, thoughts and opinions - they're bloody non-existent.

"You've got no right to talk, not even to Jurgen and especially not to my guests or clients. I don't want to hear one single word from you unless I've given you the green light. Got it? Even then, as far as possible you're to answer all questions with a simple yes or no. And don't think I'll make allowances for friendship. Far from it!

"I'm the mistress of this house of correction - and I've just pulled the plug on your right to call me Ali... my name's Mistress Blackheart! Now do you understand? I own you, Leigh, and that gives you no rights at all."

Leigh's mouth gaped. Bound and naked apart from her stockings, it was all too much for the captive and the tears that had been dammed up behind her eyes for so long burst free to gush in torrents down her face, leaving black streaks of mascara in their wake.

Ali watched her closely. She looked so fragile, and with her hair matted to her face, the tell-tale silvery trails of Jurgen's dried semen down her thigh and her face crumpled and dirty, she was all the more lovely. However, she'd have to be cleaned up if the evening was to go as planned. Ali decided it would be best to leave her until an hour or so before the evening meal.

Once again, Ali slid her fingers into her own, well-moistened sex. "The flogging you received earlier was nothing to do with punishment, it was entirely for my pleasure! You've no idea how horny you make me."

As her fingers worked with growing fervour, Leigh's pussy began to make squelching noises.

Deciding to go and make use of Jurgen's cock, Ali made to leave, then turned for one final twist of the screw.

"I'm expecting visitors later; one is a rather powerful guy from France. We've a bit of business to attend to but after that... well, a friend's dropping by for a bit of advice. That's when I'll be calling on your services to help the evening along."

With that, she closed the door, leaving Leigh to howl her eyes out.

By then it was late afternoon, but as Ali was very well aware, in the claustrophobic blackness, Leigh would have no way of judging the passing of time.

Left alone to dwell on her misery and the horrendous echoes of pain, Leigh tried to make sense of the jumbled thoughts that assailed her.

Betrayed by the one person she'd always trusted, the knowledge that she should have trusted her own instincts instead gnawed relentlessly at her mind. She should have kept well clear of Ali and her schemes, which had never brought her anything but trouble.

The irony was that she worshipped the woman. Having had the floor kicked out from beneath her and with her body lacerated by pain, bleak clarity pierced her consciousness; all she'd ever wanted was for Ali to worship her in return. But she'd never imagined that gaining that adoration would hurt so much, or cause such tremors of arousal to race through her veins at the mere thought of Ali's whip. Only now did she have an inkling of her true sexuality - she was excited by the lash, the same as when Owen had struck her.

That her need for revenge and desire to be loved should finally condemn her to slavery was unbelievable, yet wildly exciting. It was probably everything she deserved. This was a new beginning, and it was with an uneasy happiness that she accepted that her true place in life was, had only ever been, to serve Ali.

As her mind raced with the possibilities, her nipples hardened and began to throb, and there was a wonderful, unbearable tingling between her legs. Gripped by the wonderful, terrible realization of her condition, Leigh closed her eyes and fell into an uneasy sleep.

CHAPTER FOURTEEN

Having been bathed and perfumed by Ali, Leigh was completely naked. She'd been placed on a hastily erected wooden platform, situated directly facing the table in the minimalist, pale blue dining room.

Her hands were fastened in front of her, tied with heavy white nylon rope, which had also been tightly wound several times round her waist and then tied off. The same procedure had been used above and below her breasts so that the rope bit cruelly into the soft, yielding flesh, imprisoning her heavy orbs.

Sight was denied her by a loose fitting, black silk hood which fastened at the neck with Velcro. Covering her head so that any onlooker would be unaware of the ball-gag that stifled her cries, it had the added bonus of hiding her glorious mane of tangled red hair which had been scrunched up inside. And almost hidden by the hood, a wide leather collar now adorned her neck. Black, with a silver ring at the front, it had been purchased especially and, since it was fitted with a special locking device, it would be a permanent reminder to Leigh of her new status.

"It can't be removed," Ali told her as she tugged at two blue silk tassels, like the bell pulls for summoning servants in grand houses, "so when you go to work you'll have to wear a scarf tied round your neck, as if you're covering up love bites."

There was a clinking sound as two chains descended from the ceiling. Ali took the ends and attached them to lengths of rope she'd tied tightly round one of Leigh's legs at ankle and knee which chafed her skin terribly. Then she raised the chains again so that Leigh's taut, shapely thigh was held out at a 90 degree angle. Now, suspended with the lower part of her leg and toe pointing downward, she balanced precariously on the other leg. Staying upright was made more difficult by there being no supports or further chains to hold her secure.

To emphasise the point Ali gave her a shove. Leigh lost contact with the floor immediately and swung helplessly by the knee. Laughing, Ali watched her friend scrabble to find the wooden platform and regain her balance. Pausing to finger Leigh's pussy folds, Ali traced the line of her slippery slit, glistening and clearly visible due the way she'd been suspended. With her red pubes curling enticingly over her mons, she made a very attractive picture indeed, a picture made all the more delightful by the hood that concealed her identity.

Using another length of rope, Ali tied it to the ring of Leigh's collar and threaded it down between her breasts. Lastly, she looped it around the bonds at her elbows and again at her wrists, so that her hands were in effect joined to her neck. With her pale flesh dissected by the rope for no purpose other than aesthetics, she was left alone, uncomfortable and frightened in her dark world.

***

Having been taught by Chantel the importance of wearing the right outfit for the right occasion, Ali had changed out of her catsuit and was dressed in an impossibly tight black leather Basque with a back fastening and suspenders attached that held up black stockings. Her high spiked leather boots came up over her knee. Instead of gloves she wore her leather gauntlets. Circling her waist was a silver chain, from which dangled a whippy cane.

The two women were settled side by side on the sofa. Ali crossed her legs elegantly and focussed her eyes on the blonde's finely plucked eyebrows and long nose. The lips of her wide mouth were full and sensual, and it was obvious from the tight fit of her clothes that a highly erotic body was concealed beneath them.

"Well, Nina, I guess it's time to start your education," Ali gave her a tigerish grin, "so I've arranged a couple of treats for you. I hope you'll find the evening entertaining. If after a few weeks of tuition you're still set on becoming a top dominatrix, I can put you in touch with a very good friend of mine who has a wonderful chateau."

"Thanks Ali, for everything." The admiration in Nina's voice for her mentor was obvious, though she wasn't half as confident as her smile implied. She raised her leg and drew Ali's attention to her shoes.

Ali gave the red stilettos the thumbs up, admiring the curve of Nina's calf as she continued her upward appraisal, taking in the red, pencil skirt that came to her knee and was teamed with a black blouse and red boxy jacket. With a hand gesture, Ali encouraged Nina to remove the jacket and take off the blouse.

"You'll be more comfortable. Besides, I want to see what kind of underwear you go in for."

Confident in her choice, Nina's mouth broke into a slow smile. She shrugged off the jacket and began to unfasten the buttons of her blouse and slipped it off her shoulders.

In a shrill voice, Ali ordered Jurgen to fetch the champagne. She studied the statuesque woman beside her. Instantly drawn to the large, melon breasts which were barely contained by the red, lacy bra, a wave of sensuality gripped her as erotic memories of the way Leigh's breasts were so cruelly restrained replayed themselves in her mind. A paroxysm of white-hot arousal at the recollection of that delightful pale body decorated with livid stripes had her struggling to retain her composure. By the end of the evening, Leigh would be in no doubt as to her place in the scheme of things.

Ali knew that her black-hearted authority must never be thrown into doubt; no way must she ever let anyone discover her Achilles heel. If anyone should ever get wind of the craving that drove her on, and realize that that very craving was her one true weakness, her dominance would be questioned and her small but burgeoning empire would crumble to nothing. For the time being she must keep her fervour in check.

With another wave of her hand she gestured for Nina to take off her skirt. Nina rose to her feet and began unzipping the side zip, just as Jurgen entered with a bottle of champagne and two crystal flutes.

Nina flicked her eyes towards her mentor for confirmation of her status.

Ali announced frostily, "this is Mistress Nina. You'll obey her as you'd obey me."

"Yes, Mistress Blackheart."

Testing out her newly acquired authority Nina stepped forward and, with the terse command, "kneel!" pointed to the floor.

Instantly, Jurgen fell to his knees before her, his eyes locked on to her shoes.

"Stay there," Nina let the skirt glide down her legs to her ankles, "until either I or your mistress give the order to rise."

The red, lacy suspender belt that circled her narrow waist was a perfect match to the bra and minuscule panties that stretched over her mons. Her hips flared sensuously and gave way to long, shapely legs that were given a silky sheen by her stockings. With a natural elegance that wouldn't have been out of place on the catwalk she stepped from the skirt at her feet, hooked it up on the toe of her shoe and flicked it across the room.

Eagerly she displayed herself in front of the subjugated man at her feet, swaying her hips provocatively. Secretly she was astounded at how good it felt to have a man at her feet. And in that moment, Nina knew she was on the pathway to a new, more fulfilled life.

Ali looked on with interest.

"Very nice Nina," then prodded Jurgen's naked backside with her toe. "We'll eat at nine." Ignoring him now she turned her attention back to Nina. "Before dinner I'll take you through to the playroom, where you can have a taster of one of the treats I mentioned."

Rising to her feet she stepped over Jurgen and stood beside her new friend. Smiling, they raised their glasses, brought them together with a clink! and chanted in unison, "here's to a great evening."

***

"This is Pierre."

Nina was aghast. It was all she could do to stop herself from throwing her hand over her mouth in shock. She'd never seen such a thing! Transfixed, she followed Ali into the white room.

Ali stood beside the young, well-proportioned man with wavy dark hair. Gagged, his naked body was slung face down between the black, horizontal beam and the wall bars at about waist height. On his wrists he wore metal cuffs, both of which had chains attached, the other ends of which were secured to the beam several feet apart. Similar cuffs and chains had been attached to his ankles and secured, several feet apart, to the wall bars.

As he hung stretched out in an X between the beam and wall bars, to maintain his erection there was a metal ring fixed over his scrotum and a similar ring at the base of his penis. From this second ring hung a chain of about six inches long, at the end of which was a weight.

Ali gave his backside a resounding Smack! with the palm of her hand, "the leather queen demands your arse!" making the flesh on his buttocks wobble, before strutting over to a cabinet on the wall. She returned some minutes later with a candle and a box of matches. She screwed the candle into his anus, lit it, then stepped back to admire the view.

"We met some months ago," she explained matter-of-factly, "while I was abroad. He arrived here from Paris this afternoon and will be enjoying my hospitality for a few days, after which he'll be meeting up with some rather important people in London."

"He must be in agony," Nina observed.

"Must be," Ali agreed, "and his bum should be warming up nicely."

"So it's true - you really do have a black heart."

Ali turned her glittering black gaze to the blonde. "And I'm not afraid to prove it." Standing with her legs apart, she placed her hands on her hips and returned her attention to the unfortunate Pierre as she addressed Nina phlegmatically.

"I've been doing some digging, Nina. You're right, your husband's been having it away with his patients - and with a friend of mine. He's been giving her a rough time of it, so the two of us have come up the idea of paying him back. The thing is this, how do you feel about it?"

Nina's eyes sparkled with a new delight as she imagined Owen receiving some extra special treatment.

"The bastard's hurt me enough over the years! He needs teaching a lesson. Do what you want with him."

"Then we'll start on Monday." Ali went on to say that, as it would be Nina's first day as the new receptionist, she was very welcome to join in the proceedings if she felt the urge, then gave a huge sigh of relief when she declined. As much as she liked Nina, she really didn't need her getting in the way of her own plan, which had little to do with Owen but everything to do with Leigh.

Unhooking the cane from her waist, Ali strode across the room towards Pierre. She swished the cane through the air a couple of times, "it makes a rather nice whistle, don't you think?" then tapped it against her palm.

Standing at one side of Pierre's body, already covered in a sheen of moisture, she took up an open-legged stance level but slightly back from his shoulders. She laid the cane down across his shoulder to fix the point in her mind, then raised it again. In a flash she brought it down, so hard across his shoulder blade that his body jerked in its bonds and beads of sweat sprang up in a fine spray. The candle flame flickered ominously and a globule of hot wax dried on his skin.

There was a grunt from behind the gag which could have been from pain or pleasure. Regardless, Ali lifted her arm again and took aim. She crashed it down with a sharp Crack! that crossed the first stripe exactly in the centre. With joyful fervour she repeated the process with the other shoulder, then started over until she'd given seven savage blows to each shoulder.

"Has he had enough yet?" Nina asked.

"He's still conscious, isn't he?"

"Yes."

"Then no, he hasn't had enough. Our Pierre likes to be beaten into oblivion, don't you, worm?"

There was another grunt, which Ali answered with a particularly vicious strike across his right shoulder.

"What about the candle?"

"It'll burn itself out soon enough."

There was another dreadful strike of the cane, followed by clanking of chains as his body jerked. And so it continued, until she'd laid down a network of fine red crosses that covered his shoulders; his eyes closed, and he hung limply in his chains.

With perfect timing, a draught caught the flame, it flickered, and died.

Seated on Gothic style chairs made of black wrought iron, Ali and Nina were finishing off the main course of a lavish meal, expertly prepared and served by Jurgen. They washed it down with liberal amounts of an excellent vintage wine.

"She's beautiful!" Nina observed, jerking her head in the direction of the naked, hooded girl who'd been so charmingly displayed throughout the meal.

Ali shrugged, not wanting to expose the weaker side of her nature.

"Who is she, the girl that you're training for someone else?"

It was vital to Ali's plan that neither Nina nor Leigh knew the identity of the other - yet. Glancing towards the platform, she imagined how much Leigh's leg must be aching. It must be unbearable...she smiled proudly.

"Actually, she's mine, but it's not important who she is. I picked her up solely for corrective purposes. In time she'll be for my exclusive use but, as part of her training programme, I've decided she should be at the disposal of my friends." Ali extended her hand towards the platform where Leigh was displayed like any other item of merchandise. It was as if she twisted a knife in her own breast as she invited Nina to be her guest.

"As much as I'd like to take you up on the offer," Nina began doubtfully, "you can't really expect me to beat the poor kid when she's strung up like that!"

"Poor kid? You can get rid of that bloody attitude for a start! If you want to be a dominatrix, dish out beatings and have slaves at your feet, you can't have any room in your heart for sympathy!"

"Well, you're the expert."

Nina got to her feet. She circled the wooden platform in awe, admiring the webbing of red weals dissected by the white rope,that adorned the captive's pale body. Momentarily focusing her attention on the enchanting red pubes that curled and fizzed between the girl's taut, shapely thighs, Nina reached out a hand and smiled when Leigh flinched under her fiery touch. First, she gripped her mons tightly then, with her thumb pressing against Leigh's hardened bud, she slipped two greedy fingers between her swollen labia and energetically agitated Leigh's insides, at the same time tormenting her bud.

"My God, she's wet!" To Nina's delight, Leigh bore down.

Ali swelled with pride. "Yes, she usually responds well."

If she could have seen, Leigh would have recoiled in terror at the look of burgeoning brutality that glittered in her tormentor's gaze, but as it was she merely burned with shame on hearing the note of amusement in the woman's sardonic voice.

"A most extraordinary parcel of flesh tied up with string!"

"Perhaps you'd like to warm her up a bit?" Ali gestured toward the rack of canes and whips that she'd had Jurgen bring from her bedroom. "She's the perfect subject on which to practice your technique."

Nina's high heels click-clicked across the wooden floor. She selected a whip that had one braided leather lash. Her heels click-clicked on the return journey and she positioned herself at the side of the platform.

"I don't know where to begin!" Nina watched enthralled as, under her unwavering gaze, the girl's already glowing flesh took on an attractive, deeper hue from her ankles to the point where her flesh met the black hood. "What do you suggest?"

"Only her tits and cunt are off limits - I'm saving those pleasures for myself! Other than that, beat her anywhere."

Ali herself was enslaved by the sheer sensuality that radiated from every fibre of Leigh's being. She strode aggressively across the room to stand on the other side of the platform. With the need to humiliate her cherished possession as potent as the hunger to take her to her bed, Ali's veins were scorched by the fire that swept through them. Her powerful, teasing fingers closed around Leigh's nipple while her other hand skimmed over the angry ridges that covered the slight swell of her abdomen.

"As you can see, her belly marks up rather nicely. Her back hasn't really seen the lash yet, so you might like to start there. If not..." Ali worked her nipple into a hardened peak, "you could go for the cheeks of her bum. They're nice and tight, but at the same time have a fleshiness about them that makes them particularly susceptible to laceration and bruising."

Removing her fingers, Ali replaced them with her eager-lipped mouth which she closed over the cherry red tip and clamped her other hand firmly over Leigh's other breast, teasing the nipple.

While Ali sucked and twirled, Nina continued to rub and agitate until, scarlet with shame and quivering, Leigh found it hard to maintain her balance.

Then a blinding light of pain shot through the tormented girl as without warning, Ali closed her teeth sharply around the highly sensitised morsel of flesh. Leigh, unable to scream because of the gag, hopped around the platform in agony. Disaster struck when her foot slipped away beneath her. The two disciplinarians stepped back, laughing joyously at the spectacle while Leigh was left to dangle helplessly by the knee.

"Now might be a good time to start," Ali encouraged.

While Ali backed up a bit so she could view the proceedings without hindering them, Nina moved closer, correcting her stance by opening her legs as she'd seen Ali brace herself in the playroom.

She struck the first explosive blow with such force across Leigh's upper thigh that she swung like a pendulum from side to side across the platform.

"Very good."

The roof of Ali's mouth went dry as she watched her prized belonging being maltreated before her eyes. She'd expected more hesitation on Nina's part, yet she wasn't altogether disappointed. It was months since she'd experienced the thrill of standing back to watch pain and degradation dished out, and it gave her an extra buzz to know that it was still she who was in control of Leigh's fate.

With smoky indifference she instructed, "don't lose momentum. Give her another one." And so the thrashing progressed, with Ali encouraging her pupil every step of the way. "Keep your eye on your target. Again!"

With a resounding Crack! the wicked braid struck across the soft flesh of Leigh's belly, curling round to flick painfully in the hollow of her back, causing the chains to clink as Leigh's poor, abused body jerked.

"Now you're getting the hang of it."

A lascivious heat coiled in Ali's belly. Her clitoris twitched madly, yet there was nothing she could do to relieve herself if she were to maintain her air of indifference. She swallowed her lust and continued with the tutorial.

"At this stage there's no need to give her too long between strikes. Only when she's been under the lash awhile need you give her a breather. So, take aim - strike!"

The next strike missed altogether.

Ali wiped the back of her hand across her sweating brow. "Don't worry. A moving target is always hard, but it's something you'll want to master because it can be very rewarding. Get ready, aim - strike!"

Traumatised beneath her hood, Leigh's scalding tears flowed freely as she continued to swing back and forth, never being allowed to find her footing. Her poor, sweating body was racked with pain, yet still the blows kept coming. Never would she have believed that such cruelty existed, especially in one whom she'd always considered to be her dearest friend; that that friend could have cold-bloodedly turned her over to be abused by a stranger was inconceivable.

She heard the satin menace of Ali's voice.

"Try a bit lower, where the flesh is softer. You'll get a better reaction and a very satisfying stripe."

The lash caught her just above her pubes.

Her assailant's tone was incredulous. "You've certainly trained her well. She hasn't made a sound. I thought..."

"Don't stop! You can still flog her while we're talking. You were saying?"

The next stroke fell exactly over the last, cutting viciously into the soft flesh, "I was just saying that I thought she'd be screaming her head off by now!" This time there was no let up as the conversation continued.

"Thanks for the compliment," Ali paused to laugh, "but I'm afraid I cheated - I had her gagged! But it is possible to train slaves to such a high standard. I've seen both men and women have designs scorched into their skin with irons without the need for a gag, and in time she'll learn to take whatever's meted out in absolute silence, without the need for a one. Perhaps one day I'll have her branded, too."

The words swam round and round in Leigh's head as the never ending torture went on, minutes becoming hours. And all the while, Ali continued to direct the stranger who beat her so savagely that Leigh thought she'd die. Lightning exploded into a million starbursts behind her eyes as the blows kept coming, across her back, belly, thighs, until she couldn't discern any longer where the whip struck for her whole body was one seething mass of pain. And something else that in her present state, she was unable to name.

God, she was wet, so wet between her legs that she could feel her juices dribbling down her thigh. Her body tensed, and even as she swung to and fro across the platform under each terrible blow, the convulsive tremors hit her as she was beaten to orgasm. The heat spread through her body, down her leg, warm and wet.

The last thing she heard before blackness enveloped her was the unknown woman's sneeringly brittle voice.

"Oh my lord! She's wet herself!"

CHAPTER FIFTEEN

It was claustrophobically dark when Leigh awoke and for a moment she thought she was still wearing the hood. Her heart took up the rapid thumping of panic, until she realized that she was back in the unlit, hutch-like room that she thought of as a prison cell, lying on the hard mattress. She knew a moment's joy when she found her hands were free. She reached upward to feel for the collar; her heart sank, for it was still fitted in place, hugging her neck snugly but just loose enough for her to poke a finger up between the leather and her skin.

Still naked, it was just as Leigh realized her feet were also free that Ali opened the door and the room was bathed in light. Leigh was immediately filled with horror as she heard the familiar chink-chink of metal and fastened her gaze on the length of heavy linked chain which dangled from Ali's hand.

"Stand up and come here." When Leigh stood before her at the foot of the mattress, Ali clipped the chain to the ring at the front of Leigh's collar. "Did you sleep well? You may answer."

Not able to read Ali's mood yet, she mumbled a simple, "yes."

There was a quick, downward jerk on her chain. "Yes what?"

"Yes, thank you, Ali." Another jerk on the chain did wonders for her memory. "Yes, Mistress Blackheart."

"You're learning. And on the whole you performed well last night, though we'll have to concentrate on your obvious inability to hold your pee!"

She turned abruptly, giving Leigh little choice but to follow. Ali led her through the apartment, past Jurgen who was carrying dishes through to the dining ro[om] and paid her no attention, to the bathroom.

Without detaching the lead, she flung open the bathroom door and with a quick shove and a caustic, "get your sorry arse in there!" launched Leigh headlong into the bathroom. "Have a quick shower and use the toilet. Today you can have privacy but don't get used to it - in future I'll have Jurgen bring you.

"I'll wait outside and when you've done, I'll take you along for breakfast, the last meal you'll eat at my table. Afterwards, you'll eat from the dog bowl or be fed by hand. Don't look so shocked... seeing as you're not housetrained and act like a she-dog, it's only right that you're treated as one."

Ali had her stand in the centre of the lounge, her legs apart and arms stretched out at her sides, with the cold metal of the heavy-linked chain dangling between the swell of her fevered breasts.

Then it was with an extreme tenderness which belied the cruel indignities of the previous day that Ali attended to the livid ridges and bluey-purple bruises that covered Leigh's weak, abused body. Using soothing ointments and sweet scented oils, she swirled her deceitfully sweet fingers over Leigh's highly sensitized flesh in a way that was wholly erotic and, even in her present state of abuse, Leigh's arousal swirled skittishly through her veins.

Yet the tenderness didn't reach Ali's eyes, and fearing the mercurial mood swings that had been Ali's trademark since youth, and the dog whip that lay across the arms of Ali's favourite chair, Leigh fought to keep in check her murmurs and hedonistic sighs.

"Mustn't forget to do here," Ali curled her fingers over Leigh's nipples, which responded to the feathery touch by jerking to attention, "or here." She stroked her oil laden digits of her other hand over Leigh's already drizzling sex, making Leigh shudder with arousal. For several warm, smokily-erotic moments, Ali continued to tease and tweak.

But instead of inserting her fingers into Leigh's hungry, grasping channel, Ali snatched them away and strutted around behind her. In a quick movement she seized Leigh's wrists, and dragging them down behind her back, fastened them together with handcuffs that closed with an ominous click.

Not daring to protest, Leigh remained quivering silently.

Ali dipped her hand between Leigh's legs once more and sought out her clitoris. At first she used sensual, circling motions, but as her own torrid lust took hold, her ministrations became fierce, rubbing movements. She agitated the hard bud until Leigh was unable to stop her sighs any longer and let them escape in a series of whimpers.

"Enough!" Again Ali wrenched her hand away, and coming round to the front, snatched up the lead. "Just as I thought, you're nothing but a wanton slut," and returned her to her room-cum-cell.

With sudden insight Leigh realized that Ali's torture didn't consist of brutality alone; having brought her to a highly agitated state she'd backed off, leaving Leigh trembling with frustration. This was almost as hard to bear as the beatings themselves. Oh, if only her hands were free she'd at least have been able to relieve herself, but Ali's foresight had put paid to that.

For the most part of the day, Leigh was confined to her room, lying on her back and chained down on her mattress in an X, though in truth her body hurt so much, she couldn't have moved even if she hadn't been chained.

She saw nothing at all of the Frenchman, who according to Ali, would be staying on for a few days, though she heard the unmistakable sounds of vicious whacks on skin coming from the next room, along with Ali's satin, derisive tones.

Sometime after lunch, which Jurgen brought her and made her eat on all fours at the foot of the bed from the dog bowl, Ali came in with a chair from the dining room. Due to the cramped conditions, she placed it with the wrought iron front legs shoved up tight against the mattress, level with Leigh's breasts.

Stretching out her leather-encased legs across Leigh's torso, she placed one booted foot on Leigh's striped belly and the other across her unblemished breasts. Infused with an almost uncontrollable surge of power as Leigh let out a shriek when the terrible spikes of her heels came into contact with her raw skin, with sadistic delight Ali re-adjusted the position of her feet, making sure to scrape the narrow spikes across the weals once more. She crossed her ankles across Leigh's belly.

"The more you suffer, the more proud of you I am."

Such was Ali's regard for her, she claimed in a strangely husky, biting tone, that the more pain Leigh underwent the more she loved her for it. And, even as Leigh listened in abject horror, her adoration for Ali shone in her pale eyes as Ali went on to explain in the most shockingly forthright manner how much it meant to her to have Leigh subjected to such maltreatment.

"Don't forget, I taught you every fucking thing you know! Now I'm calling in what's due. Even before I left for Europe, I longed to get your steamy little body between the sheets. But what a surprise when I got back! While I was away, it turned into a real horny piece of machinery. You're a very sexy lady, Leigh, and the more marred by the lash you are, the more desirable you become. You'll never know how hungry I've been to get you where I've got you now, or how many years I've dreamed of having you chained at my feet. You were born to suffer at my hands - it's what I came home from Europe for."

She flicked the leather tip of a riding crop across Leigh's erotically charged nipples a couple of times before scraping her heels again over the savagely sensitised flesh of her belly, smiling like a she-devil as the searing heat of pain made Leigh yowl her head off.

"Shut up, or I'll fucking gag you! Just lie there and listen while I explain exactly what this is about - it's my birthright to exploit your body, and it's time you learnt that the Maitlands of this world are more powerful than the Braddocks!"

As the seductive glow of lustful domination clutched at her heart, a frisson of electricity shot through Ali's nerve endings, while in the same moment, a look of utter bafflement took root and blossomed across Leigh's face.

Savouring Leigh's obvious distress, Ali elaborated with relish.

"You, my sweet little slut, come from a long line of crooks, going back to Braddock, the notorious highwayman. What? You didn't know he's one of your ancestors? Bloody hell! What planet are you on? Your mother is a direct descent of Braddock, the highwayman. By the way, she inherited his most celebrated trait."

Forgetting she wasn't supposed to speak, Leigh gasped a shocked "My mother?"

Ali's voice was as savage as the Crack! across Leigh's belly from Ali's crop. "Shut up, I'm talking! Listen and learn. You think your mother's running a bar in Spain? Well, I hate to disappoint you, but I did a bit of digging a while back and hey shit! Did I come up with some dirt? Your mother put her pussy about a bit a few years back, rather like you've been doing."

According to Ali, Leigh's mother was also involved with a bad crowd for whom she smuggled drugs.

"If it hadn't been for my feelings for you and some of my very important connections, she'd have ended up in a foreign jail years ago. You owe me!"

But there were even more unbelievable revelations to come.

"Being an attractive woman in her mid forties, due to my involvement, where she did end up is California. She's recently opened a high class brothel, where she and her girls regularly entertain the wealthy. Unlike you, she still has her freedom.

"But sod your mother! We're here to talk about my power and your lack of it. I can't believe you were born and raised in this town yet don't even know who your own ancestor was. You didn't believe me all those years ago when I told you I came from money, nor that my ancestor was none other than the very rich and extremely powerful Magistrate Maitland. It's a pity, because then you'd have realized that I inherited his traits- he was a sadistic bastard with a need to dominate."

It all fitted... Leigh's mother's maiden name had been Braddock.

"You should've paid more attention to local history. If you had, you'd have known that Braddock and Maitland were old friends, just like us. It was Braddock's job to get the loot, and in return for his continued liberty, to split it with the magistrate. This went on for years, during which Maitland turned a blind eye or pointed the finger elsewhere, setting a false trail."

She went on to explain how Maitland would find sweet, innocent young girls who he'd torture in his cellar.

"They'd say anything - drop a brother, father or sweetheart in the shit just to make him stop. But afterwards, they'd be strangely forgiving, some even stayed on at his Manor House as serving girls. And that's what's happening here - after everything you've gone through, you're going to stay here as my slave.

"Braddock got greedy, double-crossed his friend, and in the dead of night, made off with the proceeds from his biggest job. So Maitland began to circulate rumours, and before long Braddock was captured and brought up before Maitland at the local assizes, where he sentenced the Highwayman to hang.

"Haven't you ever seen the stone that marks Braddock's grave? Hell, it's only a lump of rock on a patch of waste ground, but it's your heritage. It's not far from the railway station, perhaps I'll take you sometime."

Ali paused a moment as a thought crept into her brain. It was so delicious that she couldn't understand why she hadn't thought of it before. The image that filled the wide-screen of her mind almost had her reeling with excitement. She laughed, and her voice took on a cruel, mocking tone.

"It'd be a fitting place to give you a good flogging!"

Leigh scarcely heard as Ali went on to explain what she could expect from life now that she was a slave; what her daily routine would be. For one thing, her days working at the surgery were numbered.

"I'll honour my side of the deal- I'll pay Owen a visit in the morning."

It was early Monday morning when Jurgen threw open the door. Leigh had been secured for the night by her ankles with her hands tethered to her collar, and now blinked rapidly as light flooded the room and dazzled her.

Jurgen gave her a moment, then unclipped her hands. He had her sit up, then fastened her wrists behind her back. He slid a lusting glance over her while circling the mattress, and felt the heat rising in his balls. Not daring to touch her, he silently cursed Ali. As he unfastened her ankles and helped her to her feet, he passed on Ali's message.

"She's going to take you to work, then meet you there later. But first, you're to have breakfast with her in the dining room, then you can wash and get dressed. She bought you some new clothes."

He attached the chain lead to her collar, then led her falteringly through to the dining room. He made her stand on the wooden platform that was now a permanent feature of the room, facing the dining table with her feet apart.

"Don't move until she gets here and remember, you're not allowed to speak unless she asks a direct question." He grabbed the back of her head and shoved it downward. "Always stand with your head bowed." He gave her bottom a slap in passing, then disappeared through one of the doors, which he left temptingly ajar.

Her eyes followed him, then stared at the door that represented freedom. The insanity of the weekend drained away and her emotions began to circulate once more, and with them the inner struggle began. Surely to subjugate herself to Ali and allow herself to be abused was wrong. Here was her chance of escape.

But Jurgen hadn't given her the clothes! She glanced down at herself, noting how her nipples seemed larger and more erect than usual. Her belly and thighs were criss-crossed with a network of weals, which thanks to

Ali's ministrations would fade in time, which would probably mean she'd be due for another beating. She should get as far away from Ali as possible; perhaps make a dash for it and not stop running until she'd reached Scotland!

Then a thought struck her - today was the day set aside for her revenge on Owen!

She stood passively with her legs apart until Ali arrived. Unnervingly silent and grim, without a glance of acknowledgement, Ali placed two dog bowls at Leigh's feet. One contained water, the other some kind of cereal with milk and sugar.

Ali dropped Leigh off round the corner from the surgery, trusting her to go the remaining distance without flight.

With her teeth catching nervously at her lower lip, Leigh fiddled with the silk scarf Ali had supplied to hide her collar. As she headed for the surgery door, she had the most terrible feeling of foreboding and the blood in her knees turned to water. It felt as if they'd give way beneath her at any moment, and she gripped the metal door handle tightly to steady herself.

Taking a deep breath she wrenched the door open.

Once inside, she was greeted by the new receptionist, a rather attractive blonde woman.

"Hello, you must be Leigh. Pleased to meet you."

And she was. Her smile was warm and friendly as she looked Leigh over, taking in every detail of her appearance from her tousle-effect hair and the silk scarf around her neck to her trim ankles, attractively enhanced by the narrow ankle strap of her shoes.

"I'm Nina Brand, Owen's wife."

Leigh stopped in her tracks and gaped- she'd know that voice anywhere. The last time she'd heard it was when she'd accidentally emptied her bladder over

Ali's floor. Suddenly, it all made sense. Ali's betrayal had been far greater than she'd imagined. True, she'd told her she'd met Owen's wife, and discovered her penchant for flogging women, but hadn't let on that she was to be the new receptionist - or that she was the woman who'd beaten her so savagely.

Leigh returned the appraisal, and was surprised to note Nina's soft, sensual features which bore no trace of the hardness associated with cruelty. Unlike Ali, her whole being radiated benevolence. Yet the mere thought of the suffering this woman had cold-bloodedly inflicted upon her sent shivers down her spine, and honeyed moisture to her sex.

"Are you ok?" Nina almost purred, "you've gone quite pale."

CHAPTER SIXTEEN

Working alongside Nina all morning had set Leigh's nerves jangling and her pulses racing. While it was obvious that Nina had no idea of Leigh's identity, it was equally obvious that Ali had knowingly put Leigh in an impossible position.

With her finger curled to her mouth, Leigh gave a light tap on the door before entering Owen's consulting room. As she approached him he sat scribbling in some medical notes.

Ali would be here soon, but how on earth could they go through with their plan with Owen's bloody wife on the premises? She knew from what Terence had told her that their marriage was rocky, to say the least. Nevertheless, she didn't want to be in the way when and if Nina got wind of the fact that Leigh was having an affair with him.

Leigh was frightened, almost as frightened as she'd been over the weekend. But there were those other feelings too, those thrilling, nerve-tingling sensations that always seemed to run parallel to her fear.

She stood beside his desk, with one hand resting on the swell of her hip. She swung one leg slightly in a little girl sort of way and looked at him from beneath her golden lashes.

"Owen, I've been thinking..." she began chirpily.

"You're not here to think," he pushed away the notes and began to sift through the pile on his desk, "you're here to do as I say. However, since you are here, we may as well take the opportunity to fuck."

"Ooooo Doctor!" she giggled prettily. "With your wife outside?" Unable to help herself she was actually warming to the idea, and her mischief switch became activated once more. "What if she comes in and catches us?"

His look was equally wicked. "What's the matter, my little cock teaser, lost your nerve?"

With one hand, he pulled open his desk drawer. Unseen by Leigh he extracted a bandage, about two inches in width. With a sudden movement, he pushed her away so that she toppled backward, and told her tersely to lie face down on the floor.

Warm tremors ignited the familiar sensations in her belly. He'd taken the bait - so far, so good. She only hoped that Ali hadn't cooked up some other little scheme with Nina!

Still, she might as well enjoy herself.

"Ooooh, Doctor," she repeated as she stretched out face down on the floor, "are we going to play a game?"

He placed his foot in the small of her back. "We certainly are. But first of all you're going to tell me where you've been hiding. I told you to make yourself available to me at all times, yet when I've called round your house to collect what's due, you haven't been there."

Before she could utter a word in her defence, the door burst open. Both Leigh and Owen swung their eyes towards it, to see Ali standing aggressively with hands on hips.

"Leigh! What the fuck?"

Ali's startled exclamation was so convincing that it could almost have fooled Leigh. Except how could Leigh possibly have known that Ali's depth of feeling had left her very startled indeed, startled by the flame of anger that licked the insides of her belly. It was abundantly clear to her from the outset that the bastard wasn't merely infatuated with Leigh- he was besotted! For Ali to actually see her treasured slave beneath the heavy foot of a creep to whom she'd not granted permission to use her was almost too much.

Absurdly, that it was all a set-up made no difference now as lust and anger mingled to form a deadly potion. While hot darts of arousal shot from her quim to her breasts, at the same time her anger worked ever upward, scorching the back of her throat. Perversely, she wanted to direct her rage at Leigh rather than at Owen. It was as if she must punish her for obeying her Mistress' own instructions; for giving herself up to Owen's commands.

Owen's foot pressed down harder on Leigh's back.

Ali watched the series of expressions that crossed Leigh's face as she realized something was wrong; that there'd been a change of plan. And Ali confirmed Leigh's fears when, instead of turning on Owen as they'd planned, Ali ranted at her instead.

"You fucking dirty little bitch! You're a doctor's filthy whore! You're like your mother and open your legs for the entire town!" Ignoring Leigh's tear-filled gaze, she turned and met Owen's astounded look head on.

"I don't know who the hell you are," he prattled so hastily that his words ran into each other, "but this isn't what you think it is."

"Of course it bloody well is!" Ali's tone shifted from one of heated fury to one of frosty sadism as she tried to get her own emotions under control. "What's more, you look as if you could do with some help, Doctor."

Without waiting for an answer, Ali swirled around and closed the door, turning the key in the lock. She took a couple of paces across the small room until she stood over the devastated, prostate Leigh.

"Perhaps you should've undressed her first. Here..." she seized her wrists and dragged them sharply upward. "I'll hold her while you get her clothes off.

You'll find her completely naked beneath the skirt and blouse, apart from the stockings."

With his belly full of lust and his cock swelling dramatically, Owen was in no mind to argue. He removed his foot from Leigh's back, and smiled at the speed with which it was replaced by Ali's spiked boot. Ridding himself of his trousers as he stood up, he tossed them across the room, followed by his tie and shirt. Standing in his tartan boxer shorts, he bent from the waist and reached for the zip of Leigh's skirt.

Leigh's eyes registered confusion. "Ali. What are you doing?"

There was a particularly nice begging quality to her voice, Ali thought, as Leigh struggled to make sense of the fact that she'd been betrayed yet again. Deciding to ignore the wrongful term of address just this once, Ali switched her gaze from Leigh back to Owen, raising a mocking eyebrow.

"There've been a few additions to her body since you last saw it."

He laughed as he removed Leigh's skirt, then followed it up with a gasped "God in Heaven!" when her fleshy, rounded bottom was revealed to have undergone a severe flogging. He ran his hand over the ridges and his expression was transformed from one of shock to one of dark lust. "Someone's been busy. Who the hell..." The rest of his question went unspoken as he knelt beside her. "I've always thought this impudent bum needed a good spanking!" With the palm of his hand, he spanked her so hard that she squealed.

Delighted with the response, he set about spanking her bottom in earnest, bringing his hand down at least eight times in quick succession. He and Ali exchanged lustful glances, then Owen brought his hand down again and again, watching avidly as ripples swept over the juicy flesh.

"Friend of yours, is she?" Owen asked Ali as he reached for the back of Leigh's neck. He flicked her hair out of the way, then grabbed the collar of her blouse.

"We go back a long way," she used her other foot to give the prone figure a kick, "don't we, slut?" Another in the kick in the ribs, "answer!" and this time Leigh couldn't help but squawk in protest. With a belligerent grunt, Ali removed her boot from the small of Leigh's back.

Focusing on Ali's thin, scarlet-glossed lips Leigh answered as if they were back at the apartment.

"Yes, Mistress, we go back... a long..." her words tapered off to nothing as, still holding her blouse by the collar Owen made to remove it from her back without bothering with the buttons.

There was a dreadful ripping sound that froze Leigh's blood as he wrenched the blouse from her back, leaving the tattered sleeves in place. Without speaking he gaped in astonishment at the sight of her savagely abused flesh. However, it wasn't pity but a wholly primitive reaction that shone in his eyes

"Get the scarf off," Ali ordered as she indicated the fine silk that hid Leigh's leather collar.

Owen was quick to obey without being aware that the balance of power had very firmly shifted in favour of the strange, leather-clad woman. He grabbed a pair of scissors from his desk and cut through the fine material.

"What the... "

"That's a slave collar," Ali informed him crisply, "and it means that she's someone else's property. Stuff something in her mouth."

Owen grabbed a handful of Leigh's hair and yanked her head upward. He shoved the rolled-up bandage in her mouth.

"Good. Now, cut a length from another bandage."

She waited for him to comply with her instructions. He cut a length from a second bandage then tied it across Leigh's mouth to keep it in place.

"Excellent, Doctor. Anyone would think you'd done this before. Use the remainder of the bandage to bind her arms together."

Standing behind her, he dragged the sleeves from her arms and set about the task with relish. Within a few moments Leigh found herself helpless, swathed in bandage from the wrists almost to her armpits. Allowing for the fact that a human's arms don't fit snugly against each other while behind one's back, the job was so expertly done that Leigh found it impossible to pull them apart. Her vulnerability was total.

Grabbing hold of a fistful of unruly, reddish curls, Ali hauled her to her feet and the last remnants of the blouse fell from her breasts. Ali's spikes made no sound on the carpet as she did a complete circle round Leigh and Owen before coming to a halt in front of the trembling girl. Hunkering down, she took a breast in each hand, smiling as her palms wrestled to contain them.

"Don't you think she's got lovely tits?" her hands moulded themselves perfectly around their swell and she gave each a hard squeeze. "I plan to decorate these, as well."

Owen looked at her and for the first time began to understand.

"You've done this to her?"

Ali didn't answer as her lip curled unflatteringly. She stared into her friend's wide-eyed, terrified gaze, not sure who she wanted to punish the most. She was supposed to be punishing Owen, but on entering the room to find events further advanced than she'd planned, her first thought had been to punish Leigh for letting things go that far.

And she was indeed getting a great deal of pleasure from her humiliation, particularly from the rosy glow that swept over her from toe to forehead. She couldn't deny that she was rather enjoying sharing her possession, but the thought of getting back at Owen was growing on her again. After all, what greater pleasure could there be than orchestrating the abuse of your slave by an obnoxious man that thought he was God's gift, and then punishing him for it?

She'd punish them both and be damned!

With that thought uppermost in her mind, Ali set the wheels very firmly in motion.

"What's the matter, whore? That's what you are, isn't it, a whore? Tell him, Leigh, tell him what you are."

Leigh's pulse throbbed in the back of her throat. Her nipples hardened beneath the thumbs that Ali flicked across them as, once again, adoration mingled with hatred, and the need for sexual release jostled with the need to escape.

"I'm a whore, Mistress."

"A whore and a slave, isn't that right?"

"A whore and a slave, Mistress."

"Who do you belong to?"

"You, Mistress."

"Who beats you?"

"You and... and your friend, Mistress."

"Tell the Doctor my name."

"Mistress Blackheart."

Ali turned her attention to Owen, who was clearly impressed. She gestured for him to remove his boxer shorts. "I want to see you fuck her." The poor sod had no idea what she'd do to him afterwards!

"It'll be my pleasure," he grinned as he scrambled out of them.

She released Leigh's nipples and ordered, "spread your legs."

Too frightened to do otherwise, Leigh yielded to Ali's commands. To her shame, she felt a lazy, warm trickle down the inside of her thigh.

"Bend over."

Once again, Leigh complied with Ali's commands, bending from the waist. With her head level with her knees and her breasts quivering as she struggled to breathe normally, she knew she presented both of her tormentors with a lewd picture of her gaping sex and her tight, puckered anus.

The effect, while bringing Owen out in a cold sweat, wasn't lost on Ali either. Faced with Leigh's engorged labia glistening so prettily between her long, stockinged legs, Ali felt the torrid blood swirling through her veins. Once again she deliberated - did she really want to see Owen plunge his cock deep inside Leigh's honeyed quim? He was no slave, didn't belong to her the way Jurgen did, and somehow that made a difference.

"Ok Doctor, she's all yours!"

Leigh's terrified, "don't leave me!" earned her a slap round the face from Ali's cruel hand.

Concluding at last that it would be just too painful to watch a bastard like Owen defile her treasure, Ali erected a buffer zone around her hardening heart. By God, he'd pay - and how!

"Is there a back door to this place?"

She stood tapping her foot while she awaited his reply. At length, he nodded his head and gave her hurried directions to the emergency exit that led out the back of the breeze-block building.

"Then I'll see you out the back. When you've done with her, just wrap her in the blanket," she indicated the white cover on the couch, "and bring her out."

Rather than wait inside while Leigh was being ravished, Ali sat in her car for a while, running her fingers over the Ferrari's upholstery. How much longer should she give Owen?

Surgery was over - Nina would be getting suspicious if Leigh didn't appear soon. After all, as far as Nina was concerned, the arrangement regarding Owen was between herself and Ali's hard-done-by friend, Leigh was merely the receptionist and had nothing to do with it.

Ali smiled. She did so love being in control of other people's lives.

She was somehow relieved when she saw the part-time nurse come out and get in her car, but was at the same time agitated. The very idea of Leigh under the command of that bastard Owen was getting too much to handle. The thought of his filthy hands touching her...

Her heart was thumping and her blood pumping as she glanced at her watch. There was only one thing for it - while Owen was having fun playing his little games, she'd play one of her own. Lust flickered in her depths as she opened the Ferrari's door and stretched out one leather-clad leg. She checked her slicked-back hair in the mirror, then slid from the seat.

Almost knocking into her as she re-entered the waiting room by the front door, the young, black doctor treated her to a gorgeous, sexy smile that momentarily took her mind off other, more pressing events. She knew who he was; her investigations had revealed that he'd had a bit of a thing with Leigh. But then, who the hell hadn't!?

"Sorry," he took in her outrageous appearance, "surgery's over for the morning." All at once his expression changed to one of recognition, and the smile wavered. "If you'd like to make an appointment with the receptionist..."

Nina caught his attention with a cheerful, "it's ok, Doctor Proudfoot. She's waiting for me."

"Oh, right!" There was a look of relief in his expression as he gave Nina a wave and stepped aside to let Ali pass. Then, staying her by the arm, he asked "I don't suppose you've seen Leigh? I was hoping to have a word with her."

Playing the innocent so as not to alert Nina to her relationship with Leigh, or her whereabouts, she said casually, "do you mean the redhead that works here? I think I've just seen her getting in a car with that guy from the petrol station."

Silently thanking her cruel, lying forebear for passing on the deceitful gene, Ali accepted Errol's thanks with a wicked grin. When he'd gone, she strode into the reception area, wondering how the hell he could possibly know her identity.

"What's up, Ali?" For the first time Nina seemed to realize that things weren't going to plan. "Isn't your friend coming? I thought it was today that the two of you were going to do your stuff with Owen? I mean, that's why you're here, isn't it? I saw you go down to his consulting room. I thought you'd done something to him then. Look, if you need help..."

"It's all under control."

"Perhaps not - I think you might have a bit of a problem. Do you know Leigh?"

Ali gave a non-committal shrug of her shoulders.

"You couldn't have seen her get in a car- at least, I don't think so. I saw her go down to Owen's consulting room earlier, just before you did. The thing is, I haven't seen her come out. So where's she gone?"

"Out the back way?" Ali suggested.

"Oh, I didn't think of that. Between you and me, she's quite lovely."

What the hell was this? Did the whole fucking world have the hots for Leigh?

She pushed the thought to the back of her mind. Besides, right now she had her heart set on something rather different. While Owen was occupied with Leigh, she'd occupy herself elsewhere. Her nipples were already hardening at the thought of it.

"Look, Nina, why don't you just tidy up or whatever it is you have to do, then go home? I can handle Owen."

With a determined toss of her head, she turned and headed off down the corridor. In a tone of studied casualness, she called back over her shoulder, "by the way, has Terence left yet?"

Nina's laughing voice followed her as the penny dropped. "You've got to be kidding! You mean, he's... he's one of your- no, not Terence! Shall I phone through and let him know you're on your way?"

Ali shook her head as she uncoiled the length of cord from her pocket.

"No, I want to surprise him."

With a mile-wide smile, a fully clothed Owen humped his load over his shoulder. He pushed open the emergency exit and emerged carrying the rolled, white blanket in which he'd wrapped Leigh. Scanning the area for Ali, he made his way across the baked earth, stones and rubble of what had been the building site on which the surgery was erected.

Forlorn tufts of couch grass and the occasional wild poppy fought bravely to get a toehold between the stones, take-away chicken boxes, globs of chewing gum and empty beer bottles.

"Over here."

He followed the voice, which came from the shorter length of the L-shaped waste ground. Ali stepped out from between a burnt out van in the corner and her Ferrari, looking incongruous against such a backdrop of neighbourhood dilapidation. With her insides still glowing and her quim still tingling from its encounter with Terence's thick, rampant cock, she used her foot to scrape at the ground. She kicked away the largest pieces of debris to form a clearing, then pointed down at the relatively clear patch.

"There."

Owen deposited the blanket on the spot and on Ali's command unrolled it. Together he and Ali helped Leigh to her feet.

"Thanks, Doctor." Ali dismissed him with a wave of her hand. "Could you just leave us for a moment? I won't go anywhere until you come back, then perhaps we can come to some arrangement regarding this piece of baggage."

But Owen wasn't ready to be dismissed and stood his ground.

There was a rare warmth in Ali's smile as she removed the strip of bandage around Leigh's lips along with the one rolled up in her mouth, which she tossed aside. Caught by a sudden gust of wind, the bandage uncoiled as it took to the air. Alighting on a nearby cluster of tall stinging nettles, it decorated itself like tinsel on a Christmas tree.

With the fluttering gentleness of a butterfly, Ali's finger traced the line of Leigh's soft, pink lips. Then, under Owen's horrified gaze, she brought her head down towards the abused captive's terrified and sweat-covered face.

"I'm so proud of you," Ali whispered against her mouth before her lips closed over it. Leigh responded by closing her eyes and returning the kiss, and for a moment nothing mattered except that the friends were together again.

Owen's mind was suddenly filled with lurid pictures of his wife with her lesbian lovers. He'd never been one of those men to fantasise about two women and, quite frankly, had always found the idea disgusting. Yet something had changed. Watching the dominant-submissive games of these two extraordinary women gave him a very different reaction indeed; if he didn't attend to it soon he'd be in great discomfort.

Ali reached round behind Leigh's back and ran her hands up and down her arms, still bandaged together. From the corner of her eye she saw Owen's hand stray to the front of his trousers. He caught her glance and was immediately speared with an icy blast from her dark eyes.

"Dr. Brand," she prompted as she broke the kiss, "if you don't mind!"

With a sullen, "I won't be long," Owen disappeared back inside the building.

"Please, Mistress," Leigh's whisper was barely audible, "can we go home now?"

"Don't you want to go through with our deal?"

"You double-crossed me!"

Trust the stupid bitch to wreck the magic of the moment! Ali thought tetchily as she administered a stinging slap to Leigh's left cheek.

"Don't you ever forget that I'm the mistress and you're the slave. In other words, slut, you've got no right to question my motives."

Nevertheless, there was something about the accusatory look in Leigh's pale eyes and a sweet, vulnerable tone to her voice that scratched at the surface of Ali's hardened heart. Now that she finally had the bitch where she wanted her, in a flash of inspiration she realized that what she actually wanted was something quite different; it wasn't merely Leigh's blind acceptance of her subjugation but something far harder to give...her permission.

"I'm going to make you a once-in-a-lifetime offer, Leigh."

She reached out a hand and brushed the sweaty strands of red-gold hair from Leigh's tear-smudged face, all the while fighting to keep the quivers that would betray her weakness from her voice. She knew it was a dreadful risk and set her chin firmly to try to instil as much authority into her voice as she was able.

"I'm prepared to go through with my side of the bargain, but after all I've put you through, you might not want to come home with me afterwards. So the choice is this; either we drop the whole bargain thing and forget everything that's happened between us or we carry on as planned." Even as she doubted her own sanity, she heard herself elaborate. "What I'm offering is your freedom. You can go back to your old life and never see me again- and fight your own battles.

"Alternatively, I'll sort out the doctor for you and we'll go home. But it would mean your agreeing of your own free will to be my slave and do everything that I demand. It'll mean giving up the chance of freedom forever... I'll never give you a second chance. You'll receive nothing but abuse, discomfort and pain."

"And love, Ali... I saw it in your eyes."

"You imagined it!" Unable to meet her gaze, Ali's regard fastened on Leigh's generous breasts that heaved temptingly. She wanted her so much it hurt. Gripped by a pulsating desire to throw her to the ground and give her a good seeing to, Ali hardly dared to breathe as her lips formed the question. "So, what's it to be?"

After one, agonizingly heart-stopping moment, Leigh's broken whisper brought her up sharply.

"Please, Mistress, I want to stay with you."

"And our deal?"

"It's still on."

A tiny gasp from Ali's glossed lips coincided with her heart contracting. With a sigh of relief, her tension ebbed away, to be replaced at once by the inevitable flow of torrid agitation. The loving kindness of a mistress for her beloved slave melted into the ether as her black heart winced at its foolhardiness.

"Then let's get this bloody show on the road. Move yourself!"

Barefoot, naked and vulnerable, Leigh was unable to avoid treading on the sharp little stones and jagged edged boulders, to say nothing of the broken glass, as Ali ushered her along the 'L' towards the surgery. With her arms still bandaged behind her back, she stood facing the wall beside the door, awaiting Ali's next instructions.

"Sit with your back against the wall. Give him a view to die for." Ali made her sit on the stones with her legs open, "and remember, I don't want to hear a bloody peep out of you."

By now, Leigh knew better than to question Ali's motives as she turned and headed back towards her car. Feeling terribly demoralised and as helpless as a confetti petal caught in the wind, the sense of further betrayal was so strong she could almost taste it.

Out of sight, Ali unlocked the door and slid behind the wheel. She gunned the engine. The wheels crunched and bumped over the waste ground. She braked level with Leigh.

"I won't be far away. And remember..." an erotic spark arced between the two women as Ali told her "I'll be watching you."

CHAPTER SEVENTEEN

Owen returned after a few minutes, closing the fire exit behind him. He was about to set off down the 'L' when his gaze fell upon Leigh, propped up so prettily exposed beside the door.

"So, the leather-arsed bitch has gone!" He leered menacingly as he swaggered towards her. "Too much trouble were you, Sweetheart? So, it's just you and me now, and this time there'll be no one to step in and take you away from me. See, they've all gone, Nina, Terence, Errol - even that nice little nurse that comes in three days a week."

Stopping in front of her, he fixed his lecherously hostile regard on the patch of red hair, sprouting tantalizingly between her legs.

The first he knew of Ali's presence was when her body pressed up against his back and her small hands closed over the front of his trousers. She gave his cock a squeeze.

"I must say," he glanced over his shoulder and gave her a smutty grin that leeched unsavoury intentions, "this is most unexpected!"

Ali unzipped his fly and slipped her hand down the front of his boxer shorts. Taking his balls in her palms, with a satin, "what about this?" she gave them a vicious squeeze, followed by a sharp half-twist that brought a cry to his throat and tears to his eyes.

"Now that I've got your attention, Dr. Brand, you'll do exactly as I say. Firstly, when I remove my hands, you'll back up away from the girl. Got it?"

Not sure what to make of it, his uncertain "yes" brought another sharp twist to his balls.

"Ok, yes!"

Ali removed her hands and stepped aside to give him room to back up. "Now pay attention. We're here to discuss the future arrangements concerning her." She jerked her head in Leigh's direction. "So I'll tell you how it's going to be. You won't ever threaten her again. If any ugly rumours come to my ears," she stepped forward and gave his balls another twist for the sheer hell of it, "I'll cut these off and stuff them for Christmas! From now on, I don't want you to even speak to her again, let alone fuck her, without my say-so."

He'd seen the evidence of what this cruel woman was capable of and, realizing he was in no position to bargain, he said weakly, "and how will you stop me? Besides, the speaking part is a bit difficult since she works at the surgery."

"Not for much longer. You can expect her resignation by the end of the month. In the meantime, your relationship with her will be on a professional basis only. I might allow you limited access. "

"You've got a nerve! What makes you so sure I'd touch the little trollop now?"

Even then, Ali had no idea how prophetic her words would turn out to be when she told him, "because there's something about her that brings out the darker side of one's nature, something so erotic that everyone wants to posses her. If it amuses me, I might decide to hand her over from time to time, on a temporary basis you understand, to someone of my choosing so that I can enjoy the pleasures of seeing her abused by someone else's hand. But I'll fight tooth and nail to keep her in my possession."

"So what happens now? We just say goodbye and go home?"

"No, not just yet. I've got something else in mind, so shall we get on with it?"

"Get on with what?"

"Eat dirt, Doctor Brand." She put as much venom as possible into the pronunciation of his name.

"I don't know what you mean."

"I can hardly be more explicit!"

Once again she stepped backward, until she was level with an abandoned supermarket trolley which contained a cardboard box. She rooted around inside it for a moment, and to his surprise produced a curled, wicked looking, one thonged whip. She raised her black eyebrow mockingly.

"What's the matter? Perhaps you should see a doctor - you've gone very white! Tell me, have you noticed your hands trembling before?"

She unfurled the whip and cracked it once in the air. "Eat dirt, or get some of the treatment I was saving for the slut."

Immediately, he fell to his knees. Then, on all fours with his flies flapping open, he stuck out his tongue and gingerly touched it to the ground.

"I told you to eat it," Ali moved closer and rested her foot on the back of his head, grinding his mouth against the gritty, stony dirt, "not lick it."

There was a slightly muffled Crack! as the whip made contact with the ill-fitting trousers that covered his buttocks.

"I think we'll remove these," she tugged at the belted waistband, "push them down and let me see your bare arse."

Not daring to stand up, it was with an ungainly struggle that he pushed both his boxer shorts and trousers down in one go, lifting his knees off the ground so he could push them down his legs.

The familiar thrills and quivers in her loins, which broadcast Ali's lust for power to the rest of her body, set her clitoris twitching; power over women or power over men... both had their advantages. Though to have a man at her feet like this, on all fours with trousers round his ankles was especially potent, and resulted in her blood raging through her veins so loudly she could hear it in her own ears, like thunder in the distance.

"Get on with it, toe-rag!"

His yowl when she brought the whip down sharply across his buttocks was enough to disturb the inhabitants of the church graveyard some half mile away.

"Quiet!"

Again she brought the whip down and as his buttocks quivered as they absorbed the pain, Owen's outcry sounded as if someone had strangled the local Tom.

"Are you going to do what I tell you or do I have to beat you again?"

"N... no, please... I'll do anything you say."

"Then eat fucking dirt!"

Without further protest Owen stuck out his tongue, flicking his eyes upward as Ali came round to stand in front of him. With her leather-clad legs slightly apart and the whip dangling between them, there was little point in disobeying.

A trail of ants seemed intent on crossing the very spot he'd had his eye on, where several small stones clustered together; if he'd have carried out the manoeuvre quickly, he could have dipped his tongue between the crevices and merely pretended to eat dirt. But thanks to the ants, his plan had been scuppered.

Resentfully, he scooped up a little of the crumbly, arid soil that lay between two rough-edged, apple sized stones, and held it on the tip of his tongue for her to see.

Still the bitch wasn't satisfied, and his edginess grew when her spike-heeled boot began to tap impatiently under his nose. Who the hell did she think she was? How dare she make a fool of him! He'd make her pay for this, her and that stupid little tart he'd been fool enough to get involved with.

"Stop huffing and puffing!" There was an edge to her voice like a surgeon's knife. "Quit stalling for time and do as you're told."

It wasn't too bad taking it into his mouth, it was the actual swallowing he found difficult and he briefly considered spitting it out. Reason reminded him there were people, notably the pregnant woman who'd come to his surgery last year about her craving to eat garden soil, who'd eaten small amounts of earth without long-term ill effects.

With his eyes bulging, he held the soil in his mouth while trying to produce enough saliva to help it along. Finally, and with a great deal of effort, he managed to gulp down the first small portion, coughing as he did so.

"You see how good it is? I guess you must be enjoying it, seeing as how your dick's as rigid as a plaster cast!"

It was true. In some crazy, mixed-up way, his body had reacted to the humiliation by becoming so turned-on that his eager phallus was positively begging for action. Quiveringly alive, it pulsed painfully as it reared like a stallion. He wanted to fuck the hard-faced whore more than anyone he'd ever met. When he got his chance, he'd make a lunge at her and show her what kind of stud she was dealing with. He'd give her a taste of her own medicine. He'd just taken delivery of a new gynaecological chair. Now, if he could just get her on that, he'd tie her down and...

"Come on, be a good boy and eat up. If you finish the main course, you can something from the sweet trolley."

All thoughts of revenge faded as, trembling visibly, Owen poked out his tongue again and lapped up another meagre amount. He caught her movement from the corner of his eye and heard her rummaging in the box. Not daring to risk her wrath, he scooped up another small amount of dirt.

He heard the click! and lifted his head at the same moment as Ali lowered the camera.

"This will make an interesting addition to my collection. Of course, I'll only pass it on to the press if I think it absolutely necessary. If I find out that you've mentioned this to anyone, and I will find out, this photo will be on tabloid front pages before you have time to pee. You see, I have some very influential friends."

It was almost more than he could stand. "Ok, you fucking, supercilious bitch, you've had your fun!"

However, if he believed his ordeal was over, he was very much mistaken. Before he had time to get his wits about him, Ali placed something over his eyes and tied it at the back of his head. Immediately he raised himself up and his hand shot up to claw at it.

But her reflexes were the quicker. In a flash she grabbed his hands and tied them behind his back. Then she yanked him to his feet and spun him round a few times until he was completely disorientated. She gave him a shove, sending him crashing down onto all fours once again. Working quickly, she fitted a bridle over his head and a bit between his teeth. Then she took her place sitting on his back, bringing her knees up and folding back her legs so that her feet didn't touch the ground.

With a whoop! of joy and simultaneous jabs from her spiked heels into his fleshy thighs, they set off on a couple of circuits of the waste ground.

Still propped up against the wall, Leigh smiled. To see Owen brought low was worth everything she'd gone through, and there was a sticky trickle of honeydew dampening the ground between her legs to prove it.

***

Leigh settled into her new life easier than she'd thought possible. Kept naked apart from her collar, she was always on hand for anything Ali demanded, be it tender nights of love spent in her bed or horrendously-sweet lashes that kept her skin almost permanently marked.

Much of her time between shifts at the surgery was spent sharing household chores with Jurgen. The two worked side by side, silently and obediently, with nothing more than flirtatious smiles passing between them.

Sometimes there'd be copious amounts of spilt sperm to clear up after a visit from one of Ali's growing list of clients. And there were always wine stains or cigar ash to remove. Whips or crops had to be returned to their rack, and spreader bars, dildos and leather harnesses had to be put away.

Thanks to her vigorous training, often in the company of Cindy, Leigh had changed from being a flirtatious, chatty individual to a demure young woman who knew her place and kept her eyes submissively lowered. She walked slowly and gracefully and obeyed every command without question, and was therefore only rarely sent to the playroom.

Owen never paid her any attention at work other than that demanded by her job. Terence seemed to have his mind on other things - not surprising, since Leigh now knew he was one of Ali's clients - and went about his business quietly and efficiently. On the other hand, Errol was positively cold and rude when speaking to her.

However, the relationship between herself and Nina had grown to one of real friendship that bordered on affection. On one occasion Nina had gently brushed Leigh's hair back from her face, and another time she'd kissed her, just a friendly greeting on the cheek when she'd arrived for work.

Sometimes, Ali popped by the surgery, either to see Terence or Nina. On those occasions, while Nina and Ali would chat and laugh together, to guard her relationship with Leigh, Ali would virtually snub her altogether.

"Five minutes to go," Nina closed the appointments book, "then we can close the place up until this evening. Tell me to mind my own business, but is everything alright, Leigh? You've seemed a bit down this morning."

Before she could answer the door opened and right on time, Ali entered. Dressed in her leather trousers and jacket, for the first time that Leigh could recall, Ali had a bag with her, a roomy, black leather shoulder bag.

"Hi!" Nina smiled a greeting. "We're just finishing up here if you want to see me. It'll have to be quick though, I've got a hair appointment in half an hour." She turned to Leigh. "Will you pop down to Owen's consulting room and see if he's finished with that X-ray? I've got to return it to the hospital by special courier. He'll be here in a minute."

Leigh flicked her eyes towards Ali for permission.

"I'm just going down there myself," Ali told Nina with a conspiratorial look, then said smilingly to Leigh, "I'll walk with you."

Nina laughed. "He still hasn't mentioned you to me! I'll leave you to it and get on home when this courier guy's been." Mistakenly believing that Leigh was an innocent party who knew nothing of their secret, Nina bit her lip as she tried to convey a message without giving the game away. "I'll want all the gory details."

"Call me." Ali jerked her head towards Leigh. "Don't worry about her - she can bring the X-ray back and give it to the guy when he comes. You go on home."

Not waiting for a reply, Ali set off down the corridor with Leigh obediently walking a couple of steps behind. On reaching Owen's room, Ali threw open the door and strode inside. Once again, Leigh followed.

Owen jumped up from his seat in shock.

"What the fuck do you want?"

"It's Leigh's last day, you'll find her resignation letter before evening surgery, so we're going to give you a little leaving present." Ali took a couple of steps towards him. "Leigh, close the door." Grabbing his arm, she pulled him into the centre of the room, then stood in front of him. "Open wide."

Fearing to do anything other than obey her, Owen opened his mouth. Before he had time to realize what was happening, Ali had stuffed a ball gag in his mouth and fastened it behind his head.

Owen's eyes bulged in terror- and his cock bulged in his boxer shorts.

"Leigh, get his cock out."

Leigh undid his zip, letting his trousers fall around his ankles. Then she dropped to her knees and, with her hands gripping either side of the elastic at his waist, she tugged his boxer shorts down over his knees.

"Get up!" Ali's command was a terrifying bark. "You'll kneel to no one but me!"

"But I..."

"Silence!" Ali delivered a stinging blow to Leigh's cheek. "On your feet, now."

Leigh's hand flew to her cheek to soothe the stinging sensation. Slowly, she rose to her feet. Not knowing what else to do, she stood with her head bowed and hands behind her back.

"Here," Ali rummaged in her bag, "do something useful, Slut. Cuff him!" triumphantly she held up the metal handcuffs.

Once she'd carried out the order, Leigh came round to stand as before, while Ali rummaged in her bag a second time. She extracted a short tube with a clear plastic container at one end and held it up for Owen's inspection. Again she delved in her bag, and this time withdrew a clear, lidded jug that contained some kind of blue liquid. With infinite care, she transferred the contents from the jug to the container.

Owen's wide eyes were bulging so much it looked as if they were about to fall from their sockets as Ali's wicked intentions began to dawn on him. He shook his head wildly and began to make noises of protestation into his gag.

"It's time for your enema, Doctor."

From her bag she took a metal lid with what was clearly a plunger attached, and screwed it onto the container. Standing behind him, with the precision of an expert, which indeed she was, she inserted the narrow tube into his rectum, then pushed down the plunger. Drawing it up again, she pushed it down and continued the pumping action for several seconds, knowing it wouldn't take long to work. With a sadistic, twisted smile, she watched the blue liquid travel along the clear tube, where it was injected into Owen's rectum.

His face contorted in agony, engendered by a burning sensation as the liquid filled him up, more and more of it until he could hardly stand still. His whole insides were on fire! He only hoped the sadistic bitch knew what she was doing.

One look at her face supplied the answer - she knew, all right!

It took mere seconds for the liquid to complete its journey. When the canister was empty, she quickly removed the tube from his anus and inserted an anal plug.

"We wouldn't want it to leak out, now would we? You probably feel as if your entire innards are on fire... it must be agony. It's harmless of course, but its effect will stay with you for days - your insides will be raw. Now, stand on your chair."

Ali held the arms of it to stop it swivelling as he clambered up, kicking off his trousers and boxer shorts first. Once he was in position, she made him turn round to face the door.

"It's time to earn your keep, bitch. Suck him off."

Remembering Ali's earlier reprimand Leigh didn't dare to kneel. She bent her knees and stuck out her bum, which brought her mouth level with his cock. She parted her soft, pliant lips to admit the velvety crown, then closed her lips around the shaft.

"Come on, you can do it better than that! Hell, you've had his cock down your throat so often that it thinks your gullet's its second home!"

Nina looked at herself in the mirror before going down to breakfast. She was rather pleased with her new image. One thing was certain, she didn't look like the average doctor's receptionist any more. And after the fiasco last night, she wasn't sure she wanted to work there at all.

When she'd for arrived to open up for evening surgery she'd found an envelope containing a letter from Leigh, though curiously not in her hand writing.

Nina hadn't set eyes on her since she'd skipped off down the corridor with Ali. It was her guess that Leigh had slipped in to see Owen, and they'd had some kind of argument. Miffed, Leigh had resigned with immediate effect, leaving the place in the lurch.

Huh! Something else she'd make Owen pay for, Nina decided.

She'd rather liked the pale-eyed girl with the abundance of red-gold hair. She was pretty as a picture, had a lovely curvy figure, and, most pleasing of all, an innocence about her that Nina found particularly pleasing. Not only that, she had a soft, almost submissive nature which set Nina's pussy twitching. Yes, she'd have liked to take the relationship a bit further but Owen had put paid to that.

Owen himself had done some kind of disappearing act. He hadn't come home after morning surgery and hadn't bothered to show up at all in the evening. Nina couldn't believe that Ali would have kept him all day!

Nina smiled at her reflection in the full-length mirror, making a mental note to phone Ali and find out exactly what she'd done to him. Whatever it was, he'd not sneaked into the house until three o'clock in the morning.

Well, he was in for a shock this morning. Nina ran her fingers over her head. Having been used to feeling fine, silky strands, it felt odd to feel the cropped style. At about half an inch in length, each strand stood up like bristles in a hair brush. Her make-up was different, too. Having ditched her muted, natural tones, she'd striven for a more dramatic effect that was more in keeping with the new role she was about to take on. Smiling, she gently touched the small silver stud that pierced her nose. Ok, so she wasn't a spring chicken anymore, but her new image had taken at least ten years off her.

Slipping the figure-hugging red Lycra top over her new Basque gave her a wonderful feeling of power. Once she'd fastened the side zip of the short black pencil skirt with a split up the side, she stepped back to see herself better. God, she felt wicked knowing that beneath her everyday clothes she was dressed for domination.

"Right, Owen," she said aloud to her reflection, "meet the real Nina Brand. You won't be throwing the marmalade jar at me this morning!"

On passing her dressing table, she tossed a used cotton wool ball in the bin and snatched up the riding crop.

CHAPTER EIGHTEEN

Although she'd been with Ali for several months, this was only the fifth occasion on which Leigh had been sentenced to punishment in the playroom. Naked, gagged and with her hands tied behind her back, she stood with her eyes lowered submissively.

Following Ali's instructions, Jurgen led her over to a white cabinet, about the size of a writing desk, on the top of which was a padded, black leather mattress. He linked his fingers, then bending down he lowered his hands to form a step so that Leigh could clamber up, after which he untied her hands.

"Lie down."

Once she was settled, he moved the cabinet, mounted on casters, from its home in the corner to a spot in the centre of the room, where he locked the casters into position.

About waist height, incorporated into the design of the cabinet were several cupboards and drawers, all of which contained various harnesses, ropes and sex toys. In addition, there were two sections which could be fitted as required to either end to elongate the top. Once in place, they could be raised or lowered.

Today, only the head end had been fitted and raised to an angle of 30 degrees. Sitting with her back and head supported, Leigh's long legs dangled over the end.

Jurgen drew her attention to several sets of wide, black leather straps fitted at intervals down either side of the cabinet's top. He brought the first two straps up beneath her armpits and buckled them tightly above her breasts before buckling another pair below her breasts and a third around her waist. Then he operated a switch that lowered the top slowly, to the accompaniment of a low-toned buzzing sound.

Although Ali had had the equipment installed a couple of weeks back, Leigh hadn't seen how it operated and panic set in. Unable to speak, she made incoherent sounds into her gag. Once again following orders, Jurgen ignored what were obvious pleas for help and continued to operate the apparatus until her head and upper body were lowered so much that her hair touched the floor.

She felt dizzy as the blood rushed to her head and thought she was about to pass out, but she was still fully conscious as, instead of fitting the section at the foot end he fitted a metal device. It had three long, metal prongs, the outer two having metal attachments covered in black leather, shaped rather like large hands.

Jurgen raised her bottom so that she was in an impossibly uncomfortable position, then fitted the 'hands' in such a way that they held her buttocks about a foot above the mattress. This had the effect of raising her knees so that she was able to rest her feet on either side of the mattress. Then Jurgen's huge hands closed around her ankle and, lifting her foot clear of the mattress, he lowered it over the side and secured it in place by means of a further strap. He then circled the table and did the same thing the other side.

All at once she felt something cold and hard nudging open the fleshy lips of her labia, then as the lips peeled back, the metal, plum-shaped device on the end of the middle prong invaded her, pushing deep into her tight vagina.

Jurgen's excitement at the sight of the vulnerable girl was obvious as his cock speared upward and forbidden words came out on hoarse gasps.

"Mistress Blackheart designed it with you in mind. She may have a pile of dosh stashed away some place, but she still believes in value for money, so she had a separate attachment made for men. There's a sort of clamp that fits round the balls and some sort of ring that fits tightly over the shaft."

He came round to stand by her head. As she looked at him from her upside-down position, he removed her gag. But before she'd had time to beg for her release, he took her head between his hands and stuffed his erect shaft into her mouth. And, not having had a cock in her mouth for weeks, she sucked with relish as he took her nipples between finger and thumb, twirling and tweaking.

Once they were swollen and hard, he produced clamps, which he closed around her nipples. The chain that joined them hung down over her face. He tightened them so tightly that she accidentally bit into his flesh. That seemed to excite him even more and in a wild frenzy he pumped his massive organ in and out with such force that he almost choked her.

"Oh-oh-oh-oh- I'm coming!"

No sooner had he shouted the words than he was filling her mouth with his hot, gloopy seed. Unable to swallow it, she'd no choice but to let it dribble from her mouth as he withdrew. And, being as she was hanging wrong way up, the sperm had nowhere to go but over her face and up her nose. She closed her eyes as it stuck to her eyelids and matted her hair.

Immediately, Jurgen fixed the gag back in place.

"Ok, that's you settled for awhile."

Leaving her sticky, agonizingly uncomfortable and dizzy, with the chain dangling down over her face, he left her alone to look at the world upside down while finished his chores.

Hours later, Leigh was amazingly calm, though by now she was aching in every limb. Even so, life here with Ali had brought more happiness into her life over these past weeks than she could ever have imagined possible. The hedonistic delights she'd experienced in Ali's strange household were an unexpected bonus and well worth the pain.

And she was in pain.

She winced. It didn't do any good to struggle against her bonds, except for when Ali had popped her head round the door to check on her. For the look of lustful adoration that she'd seen in Ali's dark eyes when she looked down on her captive made Leigh glow with pride, and she'd writhed and groaned with enthusiasm to further her friend's enjoyment.

Suddenly, Leigh tensed. Two sets of footsteps click-clicked their way down the corridor towards the playroom.

"Good Lord! It's Leigh!"

Nina's shock at seeing Leigh so basely displayed was as great as Leigh's own shock at Nina's changed appearance, though it only took a moment for Nina to recover herself. Walking slowly, her gaze never wavered as she looked Leigh's body over as appreciatively as if she were a rare jewel in an intricate setting, rather than flesh and blood sadistically exhibited and maltreated.

"She's beautiful." Standing by her head, Nina looked down into the grey-green eyes that stared back at her. "What on earth is she doing here?"

The atmosphere was charged with high voltage, female eroticism as, standing opposite Nina at Leigh's shoulder, Ali traced a feathery path over the swell of Leigh's breasts with her long, scarlet fingernail. She was ravenous for a repeat performance of the flogging Leigh had received at Nina's hand, and yet... foreboding was in the air.

"You still haven't guessed?" Pulses throbbed and quivered in every secret part of Ali's body. "Bloody hell, Nina, I gave you enough clues!"

Nina's voice stayed alarmingly calm as she mentally completed the puzzle.

"You mean - she's the little slut that was having it away with that bastard Owen? She's the friend you talked about, the reason you set out to punish him?"

"You should have realized when you saw first saw her at the surgery. After all, you'd already thrashed her senseless."

Nina's fiendish smile was the twin of Ali's as she processed this new information.

"Why didn't you say something, Ali? Did she know it was me?"

"Not until she met you." With a hint of kindness, Ali removed the nipple clamps.

"Poor girl must have gone through hell." There was a venomous glint in Nina's eyes. "No wonder she resigned."

"What've I told you about pity? Of course it was difficult for her, that's what made the whole thing so exciting. That's not why she resigned though; she resigned because I told her to." Ali laughed. "Except that she didn't! I wrote the letter and left it on her behalf. You see, I own her."

"Own her? I thought she was your friend?"

Nina sidled down the side of the cabinet until she stood level with Leigh's hips. She skimmed her fingers over the contours of Leigh's lower regions, studying the way the metal prong violated her sex.

"And she agreed to all of this?"

"Not exactly." Ali's patience was wearing thin. "Look, do you want to use her before you set off for the chateau, or not?"

"Now that I've seen her like this, something else comes to mind."

There was a dramatic pause, during which Ali's posture became taut with barely controlled anger.

"Then don't piss about," scowl lines creased Ali's forehead, "tell me your idea."

"Now that I've finally got rid of Owen, and seeing as how I'm not leaving for the chateau for another couple of weeks, how would it be if I borrowed her, took her back to the house for a few days until I go?"

Jealous fury erupted in Ali's belly. However, there was little to be gained from arguing with the woman, so she merely speared her with a hostile gaze and said in her satiny tones "no. I'm willing to let you practice on her this evening, providing, as before, you don't touch her tits or her cunt. But anything more than that's out of the question."

"Alright, but I don't want her gagged. It's time I heard her scream. And how would it be if she watched the strokes coming?"

"I'll agree to that," Ali was rather partial to hearing Leigh scream herself.

Ali had Jurgen take Leigh to the sitting room where she was made to stand on the platform as before. Except this time her feet were chained to the platform about three feet apart, and her arms, handcuffed at the wrists, were stretched tautly above her head and attached to one of the chains that dangled from the ceiling.

She wasn't gagged nor did she wear a hood or blindfold, and watched in terror as the two women, both dressed for lustful domination, entered the room. While Ali wore her usual leather, the modelesque Nina wore a shiny, red rubber Basque that clung to her curves and emphasised her fluid movements. Her boots, thigh high but with lower heels than Ali's, were also fashioned from red rubber.

And Leigh noticed at once that Nina carried a riding crop, while Ali carried a very thin, whippy cane.

Ali turned to the cropped-haired blonde at her side. "I'll start," she stepped up to the platform, "stand back." She closed her fingers around Leigh's nipples, already sore and throbbing from having worn the clamps for so long, and gave each a vicious twist that made Leigh yell. Releasing her grip, Ali stroked Leigh's untidy hair from her face. "Tonight you can scream your fucking head off. Keep your eyes open and watch the lashes come. Better still, count them."

Ali drew back her arm, mentally finding her mark. Then, as the twin fires of lust and jealousy raged within her, she landed the first cutting blow across Leigh's thigh, raising an instant line of crimson.

Leigh's "one!" was like a siren going off.

When Ali had finished and Leigh's body was racked with pain and criss-crossed in a fine mesh of angry red lines, Ali stood back. Then, as promised, she left Leigh in the capable hands of Nina while she went to see to a client who'd just arrived.

Nina flogged Leigh terribly, and even as Ali took John Micklem through to the playroom, she heard Leigh's screams. However, she didn't become unduly concerned until the screams subsided, then stopped.

When she returned to the sitting room, it was to find both women gone. Blind fury erupted as she feared the worst. Searching the apartment in earnest, she burst into the kitchen, where Jurgen was on his knees, washing the floor in the required manner, with the cloth between his teeth.

"Where are they?" she clutched the handle of her cane so tightly that her nails drew blood in her own palm. "Did she take her?"

Confusedly, he dropped the cloth. "Mistress?"

"Mistress Nina; did she take Leigh home with her?"

"No, Mistress, she took her to your bedroom."

Ali swept from the room. Then, like a bullet from a gun she exploded into her bedroom, then stopped dead. She could hardly contain her fury or believe her eyes at the scene being played out on her own bed, nor the slurping noises that came from two pussies as each woman pleasured the other, sex to mouth and mouth to sex.

Nina looked up from her inverted position on top of Leigh, her chin dripping with Leigh's juices, while Leigh, unable to pull away from beneath the vagina that pressed over her lips, continued sucking and licking.

"Hi, Ali. Why don't you join us?"

Tethered hand and foot to the posts of Ali's bed, there was nothing Leigh could do but stay put. Nina, on the other hand, decided to stay where she was for the sheer joy of it.

"She tastes wonderful, Ali."

Ali, her face flushing a deepening shade of pink, stomped to the side of the bed and raised the cane over Nina's prone figure.

"Unless you want a taste of lacerated thighs yourself, you get the hell out of here now!"

"I'm sorry," Nina detached her sex from Leigh's face. Slowly, she adjusted her position so that she was straddling Leigh's waist. "I didn't think you'd mind. Look, if it's payment you want..."

"You think I'm going to prostitute her for payment? You stupid fucking cow! Haven't you grasped anything? If I prostitute her it'll be for my enjoyment, not money. Get out now, Nina, and we'll say no more about it. Go to the chateau as planned."

"Look, I don't want it to end like this, Ali."

"It's not ending unless you make it. I'm prepared to forget if you go now. I'll be coming to the chateau for a visit some time next Spring. We'll get together then for a glass or two of wine and we can maybe share in some fun there."

Sullenly, Nina rose from the bed. "Maybe I'll give you a call in a

month or so, when I've settled in."

"I'll look forward to it."

Fighting down the anger that still raged in her loins, Ali turned on an almost warm smile and held Nina at arm's length. She kissed her on both cheeks in the French manner.

"Goodbye Nina, and good luck."

"Will you take care of Claire for me?"

"Claire Rankin?" Ali laughed. "It'll be the first time I'll have had husband and wife as clients. Let's hope they don't find about each other!"

With that, the two women parted. Nina went to collect her things while Ali stood looking down at Leigh.

"How dare you give yourself to her!?"

"I could hardly give myself, Mistress - look at me, humiliated, beaten and tethered."

"But you enjoyed it! Don't deny it, I can see it in your face... and down your thighs. You've been positively dripping! You're the filthiest slut I've ever had to deal with, and I swear on Maitland's grave that you're going to pay for it now."

She brought her head down and closed her mouth over Leigh's, tasting Nina's juices as she crushed her lips against her own in a searing kiss. She flung her tongue inside the warm cavern and, at the same time, inserted the handle of her cane inside Leigh's pussy, frigging her feverishly.

And, disconnected from reality, Leigh bathed in the eroticism of it all. As the first quivers of climax claimed her, her muscles cramped, tautening her legs against their bonds and locking them painfully rigid.

Unable to scream out her pain and delight for the mouth that stifled her cries, she could do nothing but float as if above herself.

Ali pulled away and yanked the cane from Leigh's moist opening. Then, with the speed of a magician's sleight of hand, she brought the cane down across the wet, inflamed labial lips, making Leigh shriek.

"I've been saving this pleasure for a rainy day," Ali said as the blows came down thick and fast over the tenderest of flesh, "and today it's bloody pissing down! And when I've finished here, I'm going to start on those bloody tits you flaunt at everyone. You'll know all about pain when I'm finished."

CHAPTER NINETEEN

The chateau was set amongst miles of rolling countryside that included woodland, parkland and lakes. There were wooden watchtowers dotted about at intervals, consisting of platforms mounted on scaffolding and reached by steps. These were for the sole purpose of watching the ruling, dominant females at play with their exclusively male and wholly submissive guests.

They paid a great deal of money to have their dreams come true, while staying in luxurious rooms for anything from two nights to six months.

There was a strict hierarchy, presided over by the White Goddess. Below her were a highly skilled group of ladies, each one being a resident dominatrix in her own right who answered to the name Mistress. Some of these ladies chose to specialize in fields such as teacher/pupil scenarios or Lady of the manor/stable lad games. Beneath them was a handful of trainee dominants. It was from this last group that Nina Brand was about to graduate.

There were also a number of butch dominants who acted as overseers and saw to the day-to-day running of the place. Answerable to the mistresses and trainees, they were at liberty to take their pleasure with any of the rest of the staff.

This final group was made up of a whole stable of subs of both sexes. They were the slaves and trainee slaves who slept in the cells located in the chateau's underground passages. Responsible for the household chores, they were at the beck and call, sexually and otherwise, of everyone above them.

And everyone, of course, was subject at all times to the will of the formidable White Goddess.

Understandably, fucking was rife among the staff and mistresses alike, but it was a hard and fast rule that no guest was permitted to fuck the slaves without an express order to do so from one of the mistresses. This way, Chantel maintained a high degree of obedience and client satisfaction, and had a reputation second to none in the business.

***

Ali looked around her at the familiar luxury of the lounge. Nothing had changed, except that instead of being served her coffee by one of the submissive girls on the premises, this time she was served by a tall, rather stocky man, wearing a short, white frilly apron with nothing underneath.

Dressed in her long, white dress and trademark long white gloves, Chantel said, "introduce yourself to Mistress Blackheart."

The voice that answered was amazingly gruff, with an American accent.

"My name's Chas, Mistress Blackheart."

"Stand up straight, Chas." Ali leaned forward in her seat and lifted up the apron. Underneath, his thick penis was semi hard. "That's not a very big dick is it, Chas?"

"No, mistress."

"What use is that?" she said, sneeringly.

"No use whatsoever, Mistress."

"Then I suggest you get it out of my sight! Take it up to my room, and I'll deal with it later." Having had her fill of cocks over the past few days, at this point she wasn't sure what she wanted to do with it, but something would come to mind. "Hurry, or face the consequences."

As he went scurrying off, she asked, "what's his story?"

"You won't believe this, my dear, but he's Charles Osbert."

"No!" Ali was aghast. "Not the much-married industrialist, number twenty-five on the world's richest men list?"

"The very same. Apparently, even wife number eight hasn't lived up to expectations. When she discovered him wearing an apron and taking orders from their Spanish maid, she asked for a divorce there and then. It's his first time with us. He's booked in for three weeks and requested that he be put to use 'around the house', rather than spend his free time in his room, or in the guests' lounge. He believes that in a previous life, he was a scullery maid to a British Member of Parliament, where he had an affair with the son of the house."

"Is he gay? Is that why his marriages fail?"

"Far from it. You remember Lynette, the mistress that joined us a couple of weeks before you left? She had to go to the kitchen to fetch one of the submissive girls for a lesson in deportment, and found Chas, apron and all, whipping the girl's backside over the table. Lynette secreted herself to watch the proceedings, and he fucked the poor girl senseless! Of course, I had him punished severely." She paused. "Now, about your little slut... I haven't seen her yet, but I'm reliably informed that she's something rather special."

"I think so."

Chantel gave her a knowing smile. "And she's the reason you left us last year? Then, with your permission," she stood to go, "I want her brought to me in my study."

Jealously once again jabbed at Ali's heart. Nevertheless, this was her own Tutor, the White Goddess herself, and whether Ali gave her consent or not, Chantel wouldn't be denied.

"I'll bring her to you myself in twenty minutes."

"No, you stay here and rest after your journey." ***

Chantel sat back in her chair in the oak panelled study and opened her legs.

"Bring me off."

Horrified, Leigh just stood gaping at the open, blonde fringed, glistening sex before her. Although Ali liked to watch her bring Cindy off, it was always at Ali's command. But now the memory of Ali's anger when she'd found her with Nina was just too clear in her mind. What if Ali hadn't given her consent this time, either?

"What's the matter with you, girl? Surely you've done this for your Mistress?"

"Yes, Goddess."

"Then you'll do it for me now."

Obediently, Leigh dropped to her knees. She dared to look Chantel in the eye before she dipped her head. Then, in the way she knew Ali liked, she began to lick at the burgeoning folds before taking the hood of her clitoris between her lips. As Chantel groaned with pleasure she tugged very gently on the hood itself, before turning her attention to the most sensitive part of a woman's body... the terrible, wonderful clitoris. She flicked it with her tongue nipped it between her teeth, flicked at it again...

The door burst open. Leigh drew back sharply and spun round, to see her Mistress looking even blacker-hearted than usual.

Chantel remained unflustered by the intrusion. She merely grabbed Leigh's head and pressed her face back to her moist quim.

"I'd prefer you to knock, Ali."

"And I'd prefer you to keep your bloody hands off my property."

"You forget yourself, I think. While she's here in my chateau, she has become, in effect, my property. Have you lost all traces of respect? I think that maybe having a little success with your own house of correction has gone to your head, and you forget who rules in this house! Now, sit down if you wish and you'll be welcome to watch. Otherwise, leave me alone with this..."

"I think it's you that's forgotten! One of the first things you taught me was 'don't take shit from anyone.' Leigh, get out of the way."

Detaching her mouth quickly, Leigh scrambled to her feet and ran to the side of the room. Standing against the wall beside the window, she clutched at the heavy drape and wrapped it around herself, not as false modesty but as a security blanket.

Chantel sat back in her chair and made a steeple with her fingers.

"You should know better than to cross me. However, I think that perhaps the journey has overtired you. Therefore, I think it best if you go to your room."

Chantel's voice remained perfectly calm, yet the underlying authority had the desired effect as Ali recognized dismissal. As the rushing of heat through her loins quelled itself she came slowly to her senses, though she heard the words of her former tutor through the distorting mist of her jealousy.

"Take a shower, sip a brandy and take your frustrations out on Chas. He's there waiting for you now. Leave the girl with me, and I'll return her to you, safe and sound, when I'm done."

Ali gave an almost imperceptible nod of her head.

"As you say, the travelling's probably worn me out and made me cranky. Please, use her in any way you want." She turned and, on her way to the door, saving her blackest, most threatening look for Leigh, gave

Chantel a fraudulent assurance. "You'll be doing me a great honour by servicing her, Goddess. If she doesn't live up to your high standards, I'll hand her over to your staff for a flogging."

"Thank you, my dear," Chantel beckoned Leigh over with an aristocratic wave of her gloved hand, "but that won't be necessary. I'm sure you'll have trained her well."

Over the next few days, Ali kept Jurgen chained to the foot of the bed, taking out her frustrations and lust in the most diabolical ways. However, she saw little of Leigh or the all-powerful White Goddess. There were whispers amongst the other mistresses and overseers that Chantel had decided to keep the girl for herself.

Ali studied the photograph in her hand, taken shortly before leaving England. One of her favourites, it showed a naked and bound Leigh draped over the stone that reputedly marked Braddock's grave, with her delicious bum in the air, bearing several extremely red lines.

Now Ali made a decision of her own; a direct appeal to Chantel was in order. She headed off in the direction of Chantel's bedroom, designed with the bedroom of Marie Antoinette in mind. With her heart thudding in her throat, she stood outside in the sumptuous hallway and rapped on the door.

"Come."

But the sight that greeted Ali once she was inside was worse than anything she'd imagined, much, much worse than the similar scene with Nina in her own bedroom. Leigh was tied to the bedposts in the same manner, while Chantel, naked and stretched out over her, was kissing her mouth.

"Chantel! What are you doing?"

Turning her head, Chantel laughed. "I would have thought it was perfectly obvious. I'm fucking your adorable little slave."

Chantel wore a harness strapped around her waist, to which was affixed a long, thick dildo, a dildo which she'd buried deep in Leigh's juicing vagina. Under Ali's hostile eyes, she continued to piston in and out, raising and lowering her buttocks in a wholly sensual manner that at any other time would have caused Ali's own juices to flow.

"Get the fuck off her!"

When Chantel continued to thrust, Ali edged slowly toward the bed. In her hand she carried a coiled whip. And now it wasn't merely anger that raced through her veins, it was far something more deadly than anything that had gone before.

"So, what are you going to do, whip me?" Chantel said in a voice so infuriatingly calm that it was all Ali could do to stop herself from flogging the magnificent, sleek-haired blonde there and then.

"If I have to."

"Really! I'm beginning to think you're obsessed. But one thing's for sure, you're getting way, way above yourself. However, I may have a solution to this little problem." Slowly, Chantel withdrew the dildo and rolled to the side. She unbuckled the harness and removed it, laying it down beside her on the luxurious coverlet. "This girl of yours is quite delightful, and I would very much like to take her off your hands. I'll pay you for her."

"No way!"

"Then perhaps there's yet another way. Let's ask her which of us she prefers."

For the first time, Ali trembled. She'd treated Leigh so harshly over the past months, more harshly than the

White Goddess herself ever would, that Ali was afraid to put the question to Leigh. Instead, she said,

"I know a better way still."

"And that is?"

"A contest."

Chantel looked at her blankly. "What sort of contest?"

"A contest of superiority. In three days' time."

Chantel laughed. "With her as the prize?"

"Oh no, the stakes have just gone up. You once offered me a share in this place..."

"Which you declined."

"I wasn't ready. Now I am. I propose that the winner takes all."

***

The warm rays of the Spring sunshine beat down on the assembled company of mistresses and overseers, who jostled each other for a better view as they crowded around the arena. Normally used as a training ground for the long term guests who got off on the horse and trainer games, the guest being the horse, today it had been cleared to make a sandy combat zone.

The atmosphere was one of tense anticipation as the two naked women faced each other, legs straddled with their whips in hand.

Nina Brand stood in the centre of the arena.

"Ladies, we're here today to settle a dispute between tutor and her star pupil. It started over a girl, and will end with 'winner takes all.' Yes, my friends, the very future of the chateau itself is at stake. The contest will be run over three bouts. Though the winner will be decided on the best of three basis, so as not to deny you a very special finale all three bouts will take place. Ladies, I give you..." she turned and extended her arm toward the two women, "the White Goddess and her opponent, Mistress Blackheart."

A series of cheers erupted as the bystanders chose which of the competitors to support.

Chantel, tall and majestic stood with her cool gaze fixed on Ali, her most esteemed pupil. She'd learnt her lessons well - perhaps a little too well, and was truly a force to be reckoned with.

Shorter, with age on her side, Ali stood imperiously, showing no outward sign of her inner turmoil. She swallowed hard. What was she thinking of, taking on the mighty White Goddess? She could lose everything she'd worked for, plus the only thing she'd ever really wanted. Perhaps what Chantel had said was true; maybe she was obsessed. But there was no way she'd give Leigh up. Besides, the chateau dangled like a carrot on a stick before her.

This was no time for emotions; there was a job to do!

A whipping post had been hastily erected in the centre of the platform at the top of the nearby watchtower, which gave marvellous views over the new punishment apparatus down by the lake. Based on the old ducking stool that had once been used for nagging wives, this new piece of equipment consisted of a cage in which the guest was imprisoned, chained in any preferred position of atonement, on the end of the hydraulically operated lever.

Loud hand clapping announced the arrival of the dominatrix chosen to start the contest, it would begin on the first cry to pass Leigh's lips. Naked and tied with her back to the whipping post for the moment, in time she'd be moved to the various posts and frames around the course to start each round. Blindfolded, she'd have no way of knowing what was about to befall her and could therefore give no advantage to Ali regarding the best moment to start. In fact, she'd have no way of knowing how the contest was going, nor its final outcome until the victor was officially acknowledged. Owing to the plugs which had been inserted in her ears, her disorientation was complete.

Dressed in an intimidating black harness, the dominatrix climbed up the steps of the watchtower.

Ali flicked her eyes towards the platform, and felt a physical pain as she imagined life without the redhead, then turned her attention back to her opponent. She tightened her grip on each of the two whips in her hands. She'd chosen a matched pair of whips, each with one long, thin plaited cable. Chantel, on the other hand, had chosen two very different whips. One had six spiteful lashes while the other had a mass of lashes, each with a knot tied in the end.

The dominatrix braced herself, then drew back her arm and held the wicked, narrow cane high. A heartbeat later there was a whooshing sound, followed by a Crack! as the cane came down across Leigh's vulnerable breasts. She screamed - the contest began.

For a moment, the competitors sized each other up as they circled the arena, every muscle in their finely tuned, erotic bodies taut and ready for action.

Suddenly, with the power of a spring uncoiling, they leapt into action. In a confusion of fiendish blows, the two women ducked, twisted and leapt to evade the cruel lashes of their opponent while they struck with their own. It was Chantel who had the better aim, and the six thongs curled and flicked at Ali's flesh, crossing her with red weals, while the knotted ends from the second whip bit into her abdomen. It wasn't long before Ali's torso and thighs showed the evidence of battle, red stripes jostling with lines of broken skin.

But Ali was no mean shot herself, though it took her longer to get into the swing of things due to the recognition of the enormity of the hare-brained scheme. But she mustn't lose!

With that final thought fixed firmly in her mind, she set to it with vigour. As Chantel twisted to avoid one lash, Ali struck a vicious blow with the other. Laying down a terrible line across Chantel's shoulder, Ali found her rhythm and, striking malicious, vengeful blows to Chantel's thighs and belly, her mouth twitched into a mirthless smile as Chantel stumbled. Flicking one whip and cracking the other had Chantel twisting in all direction, enabling Ali to open up a deep slash across Chantel's back.

The air became filled with a cacophony of cheers, gasps, shrieks and cracking whips. Yells rose and fell as the watching crowd encouraged both sides. And so it went on, each woman matching the other strike for strike in a contest that was beginning to look like a stalemate as their bodies became horrendously marked.

It was more from luck than design when Ali's left-handed strike relieved Chantel of one of her weapons. Narrowing her eyes, she began to inch slowly round the clearing, causing Chantel to do likewise and so move further and further away from her relinquished whip.

With the grace of a cheetah, Ali flung herself forward and bending at the same time, curled the whip low with such accuracy that the biting, flexible cable coiled itself around Chantel's ankles. Ali gave it a sharp tug, and Chantel was brought down, her remaining whip flying from her hand in the process.

Triumphantly, Ali dragged the prone figure towards her. The cry went up. "Round one to Mistress Blackheart!"

While the contestants withdrew to opposite sides of the area, where slaves served them with refreshing juices in tall glasses, Leigh was taken down and moved to the next combat zone.

This time, the bout was to take place in an area used by the slaves for their ablutions. Situated behind the stable block where Chantel's fine stallions were housed, two rows of brick buildings built along the opposite sides of a cobbled courtyard were divided into four small cubicles at each end, with a larger building between. Each of the cubicles was equipped with a flushing toilet inside and a door into which, to humiliate and teach slaves their place in this society, a small, unglazed window had been cut at head height for viewing the occupant. There were no locks.

The buildings between them contained the water tanks and pumping equipment. On the outside were hoses which when fixed over the appropriate tap, could deliver a powerful jet of water.

Along the third side of the courtyard was a row of wash stands and on either side of the arch through which one reached the courtyard were stone seats set in a recess, where one could watch the daily ablutions if so inclined.

As the crowd reassembled around the edges of the courtyard, all eyes immediately focused on Leigh. Erected especially for the occasion, in the centre of the courtyard stood a wooden frame that consisted of two eight feet high uprights, about four feet apart with a crossbeam. Beneath the beam, Leigh had been placed on a stool, which brought her head up to just below the beam. Her hands were shackled to the beam on either side of her head.

As Ali took her place on one side of the courtyard and Chantel on the other, Ali couldn't at first work out why Leigh had been placed in such a manner. Then she noticed the rope tied to one of the legs of the stool;

the starter would pull on the rope, the stool would be pulled over and Leigh would fall and dangle helplessly by her arms. Obviously she'd scream, and that would be the signal. And, as Ali uncoiled the hose which was to be her weapon and Chantel did the same on the opposite side, she realized that Leigh would be directly in the firing line.

Standing beside the wall with her hand on the tap, Ali held the nozzle of the hose in her other hand, and waited. The seconds ticked by. Still she waited.

Leigh yowled in terror as the stool fell away, and immediately she was drenched in the torrent of water from Chantel's hose as she aimed it at Ali. Momentarily stunned, Ali turned on her own tap and the bout began in earnest. The women dodged from side to side, each trying to soak the other. But it was Leigh who got the full blast from the hoses. In no time at all, her hair hung limply and was plastered to her face as cascades of water ran down the whip-scribed curves her body. The force of the water on her pussy felt as if she were being repeatedly kicked. Screaming wildly as she hung from her wrists, the cuffs biting terribly into her flesh, the powerful jets swung her to and fro.

This had the effect of sending the crowd into frenzied pandemonium; the excitement in the air was so acute that some became hysterical as their allegiance switched from one opponent to the other.

By now, Ali herself was soaked, the expensive hair products doing nothing to protect her slicked-back style as it fell about her face. Unbelievably, Chantel looked as if she'd been caught in nothing worse than a light, spring shower, her sleek blonde hair had hardly a strand out of place.

The cobbles had become treacherously slippery; Ali lost her footing and went down with a fierce cry. Unable to find her feet, she directed her hose at Chantel, who came running full-pelt across the cobbles, splashing about like a six year old in a puddle. The force of the water through Ali's hose snatched it from her hands and it flew off to snake like a wild thing with a mind of its own, drenching the onlookers, as Chantel moved in for the kill.

Standing over her one-time pupil, she directed the water at Ali's breasts, knocking her backward.

The cry went up. "Round two to the White Goddess!"

Terribly winded, Ali clutched at her naked, battered breasts as she gasped for air. While she struggled to regulate her breathing, she caught sight of Leigh, limp and lifeless, being carried off to the next location.

Ali took the glass of juice from the slave's hand and turned her thoughts to what would be the final, deciding bout...

Chains were attached to the cuffs at Leigh's wrists. While one set of hands yanked her arm upwards and secured it above her head, another pair of hands did the same to her other arm, the result being that her hands were secured about three feet apart. She'd no way of knowing but she'd been chained to a mighty branch that grew out at an angle of roughly 90 degrees from the trunk of a rather splendid tree. Legend had it that this particular tree was over four hundred years old - not that Leigh would have cared even if she had known.

Some distance away stood the most bizarre erection to be found anywhere within the grounds, for that was exactly what it was; a huge erect phallus.

Normally used as a whipping post, its girth was large enough to accommodate three men, with their arms stretched out fingertip to fingertip. It was fashioned in some kind of hard, flesh-coloured material. Perfect in every detail, veins had been sculpted into the structure and there was even an eye in the centre of its huge helmet. And that wasn't all! As a refinement in the art of humiliation, it had special machinery inside and had been rigged up by means of underground pipes to a storage site some distance away, so that, when a switch was thrown, just like a real ejaculation, liquid made its way up through the phallus. Shooting out of the eye in its crown, it flowed downwards, covering the men who happened to be tied to its shaft with some kind of oil.

Ali and Chantel stood side by side, watching the spectacle as the oil began to fountain out of the top, before beginning its downward journey. Standing to the left of the two women, Nina used a microphone to explain the rules to the eager crowd.

"The object of the exercise is to climb the dick and plug the hole. Fixed to the top of the crown, next to the eye itself, is a large stopper. When this is inserted correctly, the machinery is designed to cut out, so stopping the flow of the semen. However, there are no actual hand or footholds built into the structure, which will obviously become extremely slippery. It is, in effect, a race and the winner is the one who successfully plugs the hole."

Once again, all eyes turned to the unfortunate Leigh as the dominatrix took a few steps backward and took aim with a long bullwhip. Once again, an ear-splitting scream filled the air as with a loud Crack! the leather lash came slicing down across her back.

Ali had the advantage and sprinted away, leaving Chantel some distance behind, though she made up ground when Ali tripped over a hillock. Both women reached the structure at the same time. Chantel was lucky enough to find a decent size vein to serve as the first foothold, and another above her head. She grabbed it and hoisted herself upward.

Ali spent precious moments circling the monster cock, looking for the most advantageous starting point. There was no way she could climb the thing - it must be all of twenty five feet high, perhaps more. Once she'd started the climb, she mustn't look down.

Finally, she made her choice. There was nowhere to put her feet, but there was a good ridge of a vein a little way above her head. If she could make a grab at that...

As if her legs were made entirely from springs, she jumped upward, at the same time flinging out her arms. Grabbing hold, her fingers grasped at the vein while her legs dangled. She flung them to the side, where there was another vein she could use as a foothold. But owing to the oil, it was treacherously slippery and it took a good few minutes to find her footing. Scrabbling and sliding, she made slow progress. She was sweating profusely, her skin glowing, as slippery as the phallus itself. Inching upward, she moved round to her left. She had no idea how far Chantel had progressed, she just had to keep going, upward, ever upward, her body pressed close to the rock hard penis.

Once she almost lost her hold. As she hung onto the slippery vein, her breasts flattened against the warm, oily rigidity, she glanced down.

"Fucking hell!" she whispered aloud, realizing for the first time that if she were that far from the ground then she must be in sight of the top. Gasping, she fought for breath.

Suddenly, Chantel was beside her. While moving upward, both women had also been moving round, one from the left, the other from the right, and they were both making for the same vein on which to put their foot. Chantel gave Ali a shove, and an all-out fight got underway as the two women clawed and lunged, their bodies glistening. While clutching on for dear life, they fought like wildcats, Chantel ahead on points.

But suddenly, Ali made a grab at Chantel's hair. Chantel screamed. Ali yanked her head back, back, until at last, Chantel lost her hold. With a cruel smirk, Ali released her grip and watched, as with an ear-splitting scream, Chantel fell toward the ground.

While some of the spectators surged forward to catch the fallen Goddess safely in a blanket, Ali pressed onward. There was a large overhang at the base of the bulbous head. She had to lean slightly backward to make a grab at it. With her breathing as ragged as if she were about to come, she completed the manoeuvre safely, and hauled herself upward, and at last she was horizontal again as she made a supreme effort to drag herself on her belly up the curve of the crown.

And then there it was just a short distance away - the big, black bung, attached by a chain beside the hole in the centre. Stretching her arms as tautly as she was able, she made a grab for the summit. But as she raised herself on all fours on top of the phallus, she discovered that it was not all over yet. She had misjudged the force with which the oil was gushing as it shot from the eye. It caught her on the side of her ribs and sent her sliding sideways back down helplessly. Visions of the contest being declared a draw and having the whole thing to do all over again raced through her mind. She couldn't do it! And Leigh couldn't take much more either. And it was the thought of Leigh, just how close she was to finally possessing her utterly - as well as the chateau itself - which made her make one last desperate lunge upwards, and she felt her fingers close round the chain which anchored the bung.

Hand over hand she began to claw her way back up. One more effort, and then one more until finally she was back at the crown. This time she was ready for it and knelt astride the hole in the centre of the massive slit. The oil hammered up into her quim, making her gasp with pain, but although it was pushing her up, it wasn't pushing her off. Grimly holding onto the chain she reeled it in until finally she held the bung itself. Raising herself slightly she rammed it down between her legs.

The oil was capped! Collapsing in an exhausted heap, Ali heard the shouts rising up in a wave of euphoria as the entire crowd now switched their allegiance and paid homage.

"Mistress Blackheart!"

"Mistress Blackheart!"

"Mistress Blackheart!"

Then, when the cheers had slowly ebbed away, she became aware of an unearthly silence.

All at once, a blood-curdling shriek filled the air as, down below, the victor's mark was burned deep into the tender flesh of Leigh's pale inner thigh. Ali smiled contentedly.